ALSO BY JEFF GUNHUS

ADULT FICTION

Night Chill
Night Terror
Killer Within
The Torment of Rachel Ames: a novella

YA FICTION

Jack Templar Monster Hunter
Jack Templar and the Monster Hunter Academy
Jack Templar and the Lord of the Vampires
Jack Templar and the Lord of the Werewolves
Jack Templar and the Lord of the Demons

For Nicole

I love you

CHAPTER 1

Rachel Ames knows she's making a terrible mistake, but that's never stopped her before. Even as she speeds down the empty highway, she's certain nothing good will come of this trip. She can't say why she has this belief, only that it's deeply rooted, part of a visceral animal instinct clawing away at her insides. Call it intuition. Or call it common sense, doesn't matter. Can't change the fact that it's the truth.

She refuses to change her destination, even if the rising sense of dread causes her heart to beat right out of her chest. She's committed, this much is a fact, so she pushes aside all thought of turning around and focuses on the road ahead.

She checks the map on her phone, taking comfort in the little blue dot on the screen that symbolizes the exact spot in the world occupied by her aging Honda Accord with faded red paint, bad muffler and squeaking brakes. The dot sails along a straight white line surrounded by an ocean of green. She appreciates the simplicity of the image, the perfection of it. An object moving at a steady rate along a direct path toward a specific destination. No hurdles. No obstacles to navigate. Not even an intersection or a fork in the road. There are only two decisions to make. To continue forward or stop the car and go back.

And there's no chance in hell she's going back.

Her two gentlemen passengers are the perfect companions. Silent, good-looking and only there to cater to her whims and needs. They sit together in the seat next to her, sharing the seatbelt. That might have been overdoing it, but strapping them in together makes her laugh, so she forgives herself the indulgence. This is her journey, her time, so acting odd is her prerogative.

Besides, the two of them are the perfect complements. Daniels and Underwood. Booze and typewriter. Soul mates bound by common history and mutual reliance.

The Underwood typewriter was a great find her sophomore year in college, given to her by Professor McNeely's widow soon after his very public death from a massive aneurism. It'd happened right in the middle of her creative writing class, just as the old bastard was finally saying something nice about her novel-in-progress. Mid-sentence, he'd slapped a hand to his head, made a small grunt and rolled his eyes back in their sockets. At first, she'd thought he was mocking her work, but then his back arched and he collapsed to the floor. After that came the convulsions, followed by the shit and urine filling his pants as her classmates screamed. Then, as the good book says, the lights went out and Elvis left the building.

But unlike Elvis, the man wasn't much loved. A taskmaster who hated any writer besides himself, he used critiques as an assault rifle to mow down any young soul with the temerity to attempt the art that, in his mind, belonged only to him and a handful of his peers. Sure there were the appropriate candlelight vigils and the church service to honor the brave soul who died fighting the good fight in his ivory tower, but right under the surface, the humor rolled dark and furious.

I heard that the last pages he read really blew his mind.

You know that saying, would it kill you to say something nice?

Rachel guessed it had. The jokes and her connection with the man's grisly death gave her some level of notoriety in the English department, something that had its pros and cons. The con being that the rumor mill grouped her in with all the other young coeds McNeely had been schtupping, an insinuation she detested. She hadn't been like all the others. She was certain that she'd been his favorite.

There were two pros to the rumors. The first being that others on the faculty, and even a few agents looking for newbie writers, wanted to read the student novel that the great Stan McNeely actually liked. This attention got Rachel her first agent, Hank Wells, and eventually her first sale. The second pro was that McNeely's widow had given Rachel her husband's prized Underwood typewriter.

This last little windfall was so unexpected that it would have been met with an editor's red pen if she'd ever tried it in her fiction. On hearing that her dearly departed philandering husband had liked Rachel's writing, she'd sought Rachel out at the viewing. It was an awkward meeting, but the widow McNeely made it clear that life without her husband—but with her husband's royalty income—was a welcome turn of events. When she offered Rachel her choice of McNeely's personal items it took only seconds to decide on the typewriter. The Underwood was the same one that had given the world McNeely's Booker Prize winning novel *Of God Alone* and, in her own not incapable hands, had since kicked out two well-reviewed novels with her name on the cover. One of them, her second, had even been called *mind-blowing* by a reviewer for *The New York Times*, who may or may not have meant it as a sly reference to the typewriter's pedigree. No, the

Underwood had served her well. Until the last book. That was a different story.

The reception of her last book had led to the other man in the front seat. A fifth of Jack Daniel's, making a pleasant *clink-clink-clink* sound as it knocks against the painted metal of the antique typewriter.

Daniels and Underwood. Together forever.

She glances back at her phone but the map is gone. The pleasant view of her abstract-self making steady progress through the world is now a grid of light blue lines on a white background and a single word in the top left corner of the screen.

Searching. Searching. Searching.

She laughs, hearing more bitterness and fear in the sound than she expects. She tosses the phone aside, now useless, and grips the wheel, noticing the sweat on her palms for the first time. A quick check in the rearview mirror shows an exact replica of the road in front of her, only with black, churning shadows filling the distant sky. Seeing it, her breath catches in her chest. She twists the mirror to the side so she won't be tempted to look back there again.

She faces forward, trying to calm down. Her stomach rolls over on itself and she lowers her window to get some fresh air. It helps, the air cool and sweet, filled with the smell of pine. She feels herself relax again, pushing aside all thoughts of the dark sky behind her.

The Honda eats up mile after mile, straight as could be. Tall pines on either side of the road create a corridor that feels somehow both majestic and claustrophobic. A couple of checks of the phone shows the fancy map is out for good, but she's made her peace with that. She has the simple directions in her head.

But that's what scares her. Wasn't life simple? Just a few simple rules to follow. Treat others as you want to be treated. Tell the truth. Do the right thing. Only kill what you intend to eat. Keep those you love safe. Don't wear white after Labor Day. Don't pee in the pool.

Simple enough instructions, as clear-cut as the road down which she now travels. But the one thing she's proven over and over in her life is that she's capable of violating the simplest of rules. Even unintentionally. So, even on a straight road with no turns and no decisions to make, she knows she's still right on the edge of being lost. She feels as if she's teetering, balanced on so fine an edge that she's at the mercy of the direction of the next breeze.

If she were to get lost, the certainty that she would never find her way back again coils around her heart and lungs and squeezes tighter with each thump of her tires along the highway.

You're not going farther, you're going deeper, says a voice in her head.

Not farther, deeper.

It's a ridiculous notion. She's in a car, on a road, with a place to go and directions to get there. Everything else is noise.

Her phone has it all wrong. She isn't searching, searching, searching as it insists. Its little electrodes and transistors might be panicked from losing touch with the outside world, but it's exactly what Rachel wants.

Consequences be damned.

CHAPTER 2

The tires crunch the gravel driveway in a
satisfying way as she pulls up to the cabin. The
sound draws out a memory of summers in New
England. Only the gravel was seashells then,
millions of them, smashed up and laid down as
filler for their family vacation home. Rachel shakes
her head, erasing the thought. No memories. Not
now.

She parks the Honda and looks over her
new home. It isn't much, just a simple cabin, four
walls of weathered clapboard on a raised
foundation. The wood is grey and bare except for a
few small patches of stubborn flaking paint, likely
white at one time, but aged with grime that makes

it the same color as decayed teeth. There are long smears of rust from dozens of nail heads that look like draining bullet wounds. Bushes and trees push in on the structure from all sides. Vines cover the south wall, tentacles stretching from ground to roof, fingers dug into the seams between the boards, prying into them and buckling them outward. It looks as if the forest has been caught in the act of choking the cabin to death right before she showed up and ruined all the fun.

"Lovely," she says, opening her car door. She points to Underwood and Daniels. "You boys stay here. I'll check things out."

She closes the door and presses her key fob, chirping the locks. It's a ridiculous notion as she doubts there is anyone around for miles. But some things are hard-wired into her. A decade of living in New York doesn't leave a person unscathed.

She walks up to the gate on the picket fence that stretches across the front of the house. She marvels how it hangs slanted on its hinges and creaks back and forth in the breeze in a perfect horror movie way. It makes her smile. As does the bleached white bull's skull sitting on a rock next to it, thick horns arching up over its cracked bones and vacant, staring eye sockets. Her kind of place.

She nudges the gate open and walks through.

There's a door halfway down the length of the wall. Because of the raised foundation, there are old, crooked stairs that lead up to a small landing. The wood creaks in protest as she puts her weight on the first step and tests whether it will hold her. She's not so sure. From where she stands she can see that the top section of the door was a screen at one time, but it's so shredded and baked by the sun that it looks more like a nest of spiderwebs hanging there. Through the hole she sees the heavier interior door with four window panes. This door's cracked open, which surprises her.

"Hello?" she calls out. She looks at her watch. She's early but the person she's meeting must have arrived before her. But there hadn't been a car. None that she'd seen anyway. "Anyone there?"

Only the wind answers, rustling through the trees that sway in a slow dance overhead. The frayed strands of the screen lift into the air briefly, then resettle. The interior door doesn't move.

It would make sense to walk up the three stairs and knock on the door, but something about the whole situation bothers her. She walks past the door and heads around back.

The cabin is right on the water's edge of the lake and, as far as main attractions go, this one doesn't disappoint. A small grass yard, surprisingly cut down so it looks like a plot of green suburbia right there in the wild, stretches the thirty feet from the deck attached to the back of the cabin down to the water. It is a gentle slope, which explains the need for the cabin's raised foundation. A floating dock extends like a single finger into the water and ends with a rectangular platform on which sits a single Adirondack chair. She spies a canoe off to the side, stored upside-down, weeds growing up around it.

But the view beyond the pier is the star of the show. The lake is deserted, the wooded shoreline unbroken by another cottage as far as she can see. Gone are the evergreen pines from the drive down, replaced by the riotous colors of the birch and elm in the peak of their fall transformations. The sun has dropped low on the horizon and sets the forest on fire, sparking a thousand diamonds on the lake surface rippled from the breeze.

"Can I help you?" a man's voice says to her left.

She's so taken in by the view that she doesn't even turn.

"I don't think you can," she whispers.

"Will you let me try?" he asks.

She turns as the man walks up from the water, a form silhouetted by the sun. She squints to get a look at him, feeling a tingle of anticipation, hoping.

"I don't tend to accept help from strangers," she says.

"And I tend not to rent my cabin to them. First time for everything, as they say."

"Who says?"

"What's that?"

"Who says first time for everything?"

The man shrugs and steps forward. "Just people."

He wears blue jeans and a flannel with rolled sleeves. A few days of beard growth covers his face, but it makes him look rustic, unlike those pretentious fakes in men's magazines. Although she figures his strong jaw and blue eyes alone could have gotten him work in one of those publications if he wanted it.

He holds out his hand. "Name's John."

She takes his hand and shakes it, noticing it's softer than she imagined which puts his whole outdoorsy look into question.

"Rachel," she says.

He smiles like her name is a snippet of attractive music.

"What do you think of the place?" he asks. "Will it work?"

She looks back out over the water. It's exactly what she needs, the place she would paint as her perfect spot if she had any skill with a brush at all. "It's fine," she says.

He grins as if he can see right through her and knows she's dying to sit in the chair on the dock, feel the wind on her skin, the sun on her face. Just her, a notebook and Mother Nature in all of her soothing grace.

"Okay, it's more than fine. It's perfect," she says.

He likes the comment, his eyes smiling as he looks around as if just seeing the view for the first time. "It's a good place," he says. Then he turns to the cabin. "It could use a little fixing up, but it'll keep the rain out. Well, in most places that is."

"The more rustic the better."

"That's what you said on the phone." He points to the side of the cabin. "There's a generator if you really need it, but it's loud and kind of messes with the whole peace and quiet thing. There's propane for cooking. A couple of lanterns and a ton of candles you're welcome to use."

"Sounds great."

"Can I help you get your luggage?"

She shakes her head. "I only have a small bag and a typewriter." She doesn't mention her bottle of Jack.

"Are you a writer or something?"

"Or something," she replies, immediately feeling rude. "Yeah, I do some writing."

"This is a good place for it," he says. "This place can work, if you give it a fair try."

She blinks hard. She smells something burning. There's noise. The crackle and spit of a fire. She turns hard to look over her shoulder, actually hoping a fire has started behind her. But she knows better. The noise is always there in the background. Only now it's asserting itself. Rising decibel by decibel until it's a roar. There are voices in the sound. Shouts. Screaming.

"Are you okay?" John asks.

The sound turns off like a switch has been flipped. She stands there, breathing hard, her legs trembling.

"I said are you okay?"

She looks up at him, the blue eyes of this stranger that are so full of concern that it nearly makes her cry. She says the only thing she can under their scrutiny.

"I don't really know."

CHAPTER 3

Rachel watches John's truck disappear down the lane. She doesn't remember seeing his vehicle when she parked her own, but she doesn't think much of it. She's not exactly on top of her game and she knows it. As she watches the taillights grow smaller, she is surprised to feel disappointment at being left alone. She turns back to the cabin, holding her arms across her chest as the wind blows colder. The sun is lower in the sky, muting the hues of the world around her. Even the lake that appeared vibrant and filled with life when she first arrived now looks brown and sluggish, lapping at the dirt edges of the shore.

As she gazes across the water, she's struck by the sight of a second cabin on the far side of the lake. She doesn't know how she could have missed it before. It's plain enough to see. A single story cabin made of rough logs. It has only a few windows and these are small and widely spaced, so different from the modern style with walls of glass to maximize a view. This cabin was built for utility and bears no resemblance to the wide-open structures built by damn fools who'd never had to survive a harsh New England winter. There's a campfire in front of the cabin and a trail of white smoke spiraling up into the sky.

She squints and thinks she can make out the shape of a person wrapped in a blanket sitting on the far side of the flames. It's a good distance away, maybe a quarter mile across, and it's growing darker, so she can't be sure. But it feels like someone's there. It feels like someone's watching her.

She shivers and hates herself for the weakness. So what if someone was watching her? She was watching them too, right?

"Hey!" she calls out, raising her arm in a wave. "Hello."

It's meant as an act of bravery, but her voice is swallowed up by the world, carried away on the wind and lost among the trees. She lowers her arm, feeling small and alone. She wonders for the first time whether coming to this place had been a mistake. Turning her back on the stranger watching her, she walks inside.

16

It's dark in the cabin and the light switches don't work. John-the-landlord gave her the five-cent tour and showed her how to work the generator outside, even offering to leave it on after he demonstrated how to start it. The thing had growled and shook like it might blow up, so she'd assured him that she'd be fine without it. But after fumbling around in the dark for a few minutes, she thinks the noise would have been a small price for the convenience of a light switch that worked.

Once she finds the lantern and gets it going, the cabin fills up with all the light she needs. She grabs her duffle bag out of the bedroom and brings it out into the living room. Underwood already waits for her in the middle of the table, an optimistic stack of blank paper next to him. Earlier, she'd moved the other three chairs from around the table into the second bedroom so that it felt more like a desk. The single chair faces the sliding glass doors and the view of the lake, now just dark outlines of the hills to the west.

She empties the contents of the duffle onto the table. A couple pairs of jeans, some shirts and sweaters. Underwear. Toothbrush. Then something heavy wrapped in a thick cloth hits the table with a dull thud.

She holds the object in her hand. Of course she knows what it is. It's hers after all, but still the sensation of holding it makes her pause. There's nothing else in the world that feels quite the same as a loaded gun.

Carefully, she unwinds the cloth around it, not willing to bet that she'd put the safety on when she'd packed it. The fact that she can't remember putting it in her bag at all isn't a good sign.

Pulling back the last layer of the cloth, she gives a low whistle. It's a beautiful thing to behold. Blued steel. Oiled so the surface glistens. Crosshatch pattern on the handle. She releases the magazine and catches it as it slides out. It's full, all fifteen rounds accounted for. Something seems wrong about that, but she can't quite put her finger on what it might be. As she's thinking it through, she hears the first wolf howl.

It's a forlorn sound, high-pitched and aching. Seconds later, it's joined by another voice. And then another. She slides open the glass door and steps out onto the deck, pushing the magazine back into the gun. The wolves are some distance off, at least as far as she can tell, but they are putting on a show. She closes her eyes and listens to the sound, the way the howls rise together until they reach a pitch, and then hang suspended in a single pure note. There's language in the sound, she can sense it. And the language is filled with grief and pain and regret.

A vicious snarl erupts right in front of her. Her eyes bolt open and she raises her gun, pointing wildly into the dark. The snarl turns into a barking sound, only there's something wrong. It's unnatural. Almost comical.

Then the sound turns into laughter. As she watches, a man walks out of the dark, hands up in the air, grinning like a tomcat.

"You should see your face," the man says. "Looks like you just shit yourself."

The man's old, early seventies maybe, with short spiked grey hair that twists in all directions. His face looks emaciated, the skin stretched so tight against his skull that it looks like it might tear. The lantern casts deep shadows, turning his eye sockets into dark holes. But for his age, the man's body is surprisingly muscled, coiled tight as if ready at any minute for violence.

"What the fuck was that?" she says.

"Take it easy," he says, smiling with yellow tobacco-stained teeth. "Didn't mean nothing by it."

She waves her gun in the air. "You're lucky I didn't shoot you."

"Got a gun, huh? Good. Everyone ought to have a gun." He lifts his soiled denim work shirt and shows a gun sticking out from his waistband. Behind the gun, she sees a jagged scar that runs in a convoluted pattern from the man's abdomen, up through his navel, then disappears under his shirt. It's like no scar she's ever seen. Whatever hacked the man's body open, it hadn't been a scalpel. That much was certain.

"Are you the neighbor?" she asks, aware that her finger continues to brush back and forth across her gun's safety. "From across the lake?"

The man grins and it makes her shiver. "That's right. I'm your neighbor. Has a nice ring to

19

it, don't you think?" He pauses only briefly, jumping into the space normally reserved for someone to carry their half of the conversation. "Name's Granger. Horace Granger." He points to the cabin. "You like the place?"

"Just got here today."

"That's no answer."

"Look, it's late. You got me at a bad time," she says. "Maybe we can talk in a couple days after I get settled. Or next week?"

"You heard the wolves, didn't you?" Granger's voice drops in register. The fake home-cooking, good-ol' boy grin is gone and he examines her with a level of interest that makes the hairs on her arms stand on end. The look makes her feel exposed. She crosses her arms in front of her like the old man just caught her stepping out of the shower. She doesn't answer. "That's OK. I thought you might hear them. Scary at first, but they won't hurt you. Unless you let them, of course."

"Why would I let them?" she asks, hating the quiver in her voice. There's something about this man that has her on her heels.

"Seems that's a question only you can answer," he says. "But I suggest you figure it out sooner than later. This here's the hungry season. And that's the truth."

A sudden stab of memory from her childhood strikes her. A day at the zoo with her dad, probably when she was eight or nine. She knew from her many trips before that the lion was usually asleep in the back cage, always to her disappointment. But on one day, the lion was wide awake, pacing back and forth in its enclosure. Eyes bright. Coat twitching at every sound and smell. It looked right at her, safely on the other side of a moat and a fence, and yet she knew without question that the creature wanted to kill her. To run her down, sink its claws into her back and drag her to the ground. It wanted to feed on her flesh, drink up her salty blood, chew on her rib bones until they cracked open and gave up the juicy marrow inside. All this she knew with a look into the creature's eyes.

Granger fixes his eyes on her the same exact way. And there's no moat or fence between them.

"Thanks for the advice," she says. "I'll be on the lookout. Be safe on your way back."

Most people take such an overt hint, but Granger is clearly not most people. He takes a deep breath and looks around as if taking in his surroundings for the first time. He produces a silver flask from his back pocket and holds it out to her.

"No thanks," she says.

"Do you mind if I..." He holds up the flask.

I don't give a shit what you do, just as long as you do it while you're getting your ass to your side of the lake, is what she wants to say. Instead, she motions for him to go ahead.

He unscrews the cap and raises the flask in a salute. "To hell with the wolves," he says before putting the flask to his lips and suckling it greedily.

21

Brown fluid dribbles from the corners of his mouth and he doesn't bother wiping it away. When he lowers the flask, he gives an extra long contented sigh.

"I don't want to be rude," she says.

"Which is what people say right before being rude," Granger says. "I might be old as shit, but I'm not dumb as a turd. I can see you want me to move along. And that's fine," he says, his eyes taking a tour of her body. "Fine, indeed."

She holds up her hand, the one with the gun. It's not pointed at him, but she means it as a reminder. "See you around." She turns, walks to the sliding door and opens it. She's about to walk inside when Granger calls out.

"Just one word of warning about the cabin," he says.

It's tempting to just ignore the man and walk inside, but something in his voice makes her stop. He has one arm up in the air, a bony hand that's not much more than a claw pointing at her new home. "When it tries to tell you something, just be careful. It won't always be the truth."

With that, Granger walks away, the night swallowing him up so quickly that she wonders for a second if she dreamt the whole thing. If she'd been drinking, she might have lingered on that idea a bit longer. But she hasn't started yet. She decides that might be the problem.

She walks into the house, slams the slider shut and checks the lock. She walks past the table and gives Underwood the middle finger, finds it lacking, so doubles it up with her other hand. Underwood sits there, sturdy, unflinching, patient. His worst qualities.

She grabs her bottle of Jack, skips the glass and goes right for a long, satisfying pull from the bottle. She feels the tickle of whiskey dripping from the corners of her mouth, but she wipes it away. She's not a Goddamned animal.

The drink calms her nerves and she swallows another mouthful, hearing a song in her head, oddly voiced by young children as if they were jumping rope.

One is good,
Two is best,
Three puts Mommy down to rest.

The whiskey goes down like water. Good thing she knows the song up to the number twenty. She pours the Jack into the glass for the next one, like that will slow her down enough to make a difference.

Four is cool,
Five is tight,
Six makes Mommy feel all right.

The song goes on and on. And as she sings it, the wolves stay quiet. And the cabin doesn't say a word.

CHAPTER 4

"Hello, miss?" a man's voice says.

Rachel opens her eyes slowly and squints against the bright sunlight. A shadow looms over her, a head with a halo. An angel, maybe?

"It's John," he says, ending the mystery. "Are you all right?"

She raises herself up on an elbow. She's out on the deck, a blanket from the bedroom bunched beneath her and pillows from the couch piled up near her head. She has no recollection of moving her party outside the night before. It seems odd that she'd have chosen to leave the cabin, especially after that freak show Granger had shown up. But there she was, sprawled out in the same clothes she'd been wearing the day before.

"Yeah, I'm fine," she says.

"You know, you rented the whole cabin. You're free to use either of the bedrooms," he says.

She climbs to her feet. "No one likes a smartass, John. That's just one of those truths in the world. Like—"

"Like don't pee in the pool?" he asks.

She nods. That's something she says all the time. Granted, it isn't terribly original, but it's still odd to hear one of her sayings parroted back at her. She ignores it as coincidence. "Anyway, I slept outside to see the stars. Beautiful."

John looks up to the sky. "Pretty cloudy last night," he says. "Don't think there were many stars out."

"And your point is?"

John holds up his hands. "If you were watching the stars then you were watching the stars. Who am I to argue?"

"Exactly." She stares down at the two grocery bags on the deck next to him. "You moving in?"

"No, I just thought you could use a few supplies. Just the basics. Bread, milk, eggs, sausage. The usual."

"You do this for all your renters?"

"Just the ones who look like they could use the help."

She finds herself annoyed and charmed all at once. "I thought you New Englander-types were good about staying out of other people's business. Keeping your Yankee selves to yourselves."

He grins. "Who said I'm from here? So what's it going to be? Do I take this stuff home with me or can I cook you up some breakfast?"

Her stomach growls as if to voice its vote. She hates to admit it, but she's famished. "Well, technically, it's your place."

"I'll take that as a *yes please*," he says. "If you'd like to use the shower, there's hot water."

"Is that a hint?"

"Take it any way you want to," John calls over his shoulder as he carries the groceries into the cabin. "Just saying there's soap and shampoo with your name on it."

She knows she ought to be offended, but a whiff of the shirt she's wearing and she knows he's right. She follows him into the cabin. Underwood remains unmoved from the night before, the little stack of blank pages still there. No author elves have shown up overnight to hammer out the next Great American Novel. Hell, after the reception of her last book she'd make do with an Amazon bestseller in some weird, random category that no one had ever heard of. Something like Kindle—Literature—American author—Suspense—Tragedy—Written While Hammered—Somewhat Incoherent—Epic. The sad truth was that a category like that probably existed and her last book hadn't even shown up there.

The shower feels better than she expects. She intended to make it quick since she didn't trust the hot water heated by the single solar panel out back to last very long. But once in, she luxuriates in the waves of steam trapped in the small bathroom. The coarse bar soap exfoliates layers of her skin, scraping away the outermost layer of herself. She rubs until her skin glows pink and wonders if she kept going whether the bar of soap would eventually act as an eraser and just erase her out of existence all together. The thought's tempting, but the abrupt end of the hot water sends her jumping from the shower.

By the time she's dressed in new clothes and has towel dried her hair to an acceptable level, the cabin's filled with the smells of breakfast. When she walks out, John already has scrambled eggs, bacon, toast and sliced oranges plated.

"Coffee?" he asks.

"Sure," she says, poaching a piece of bacon from one of the plates.

He pours some milk and a teaspoon and a half of sugar into a mug, fills it with steaming coffee, then hands it to her. She takes a sip and savors the dark roasted taste in her mouth. Sometimes the first cup of coffee in the morning is better than a week of orgasms.

"Good coffee," she says. "How'd you know how I take it? Down to putting the milk and sugar in first?"

John shrugs. "That's how I take it. Just a habit."

"Uh-huh," she says, spying the black coffee in his cup. He sees her notice and looks away, caught in the lie. She feels a chill, like a stranger's fingers have touched her skin. She wonders how he knew this detail about her and, even more strange, why he would lie about it. But it's just a cup of coffee, not exactly earth-shattering mindreading skills on display. Likely just another coincidence, the way some ex-lover liked her coffee prepared. He looks embarrassed enough that he was caught lying that she lets it go. "Should we eat outside?" she asks.

"You mean in your bedroom?"

"Remember that whole thing about smartasses?"

They go outside and sit opposite one another on the rickety picnic bench on the deck. She has the better seat facing the lake but she hardly notices it. Once she starts in on her breakfast she eats through it like it's her first meal in months.

"Saw your typewriter," John says, his mouth full of eggs. "That's pretty old school."

"It belonged to a friend of mine. I inherited it after his death." It was mostly true, so much so that she doesn't even feel a pang at the little white lies inside of it.

"I'm sorry to hear that."

She washes down her toast with long slugs of the coffee, then shrugs. "It was a while ago. Time has a way of smoothing the edges on things like that."

John puts his coffee down. "You think that's true?"

JEFF GUNHUS

She considers the idea and sees the need in John's face that hadn't been there seconds earlier. So caught up in her own mess, she hasn't even thought to consider why a good-looking guy like her new landlord is living up in the middle of nowhere. There can't be much of a social life up here. No good-looking women to chase. No office to go to for some hard-charging career. No, he's out in the wilderness just like she is. And she recognizes the look in his eye as the same one she sees in the mirror each day.

He looks like he wants a real answer, so she gives him one. "I think time rubs down the edges, sure. But it's like this picnic bench we're on. Someone sanded this thing at some point. The weather and time wore it down a little more. But it's still here. It's still a bench. And when you least expect it to, it's still capable of lodging a major splinter right up your ass."

John bursts out laughing, little pieces of egg spraying from his mouth. Fortunately, his reflexes are good enough to turn away from her first.

"I'm sorry," he says, wiping his mouth. "I didn't see that coming."

"I'm here to please," she says. "Be here all week. Tip your waitress."

"You paid for three months, so you're welcome to stay here longer than a week. Up to you."

She doesn't remember paying, or for how long. The disturbing idea that she can't recall the transaction sticks with her for a second, but then

29

she lets it go. Her friend Jack has been around a lot in the last few months, so forgetting things unfortunately isn't an uncommon occurrence for her. Besides, three months seems like a good amount of time to her. She looks out over the lake, wondering if this place will be different than the others she's tried, or if it'll all end the same way. More blank pages. More frustration.

"I wanted to warn you about your one neighbor on the lake," John says. "He's kind of a character."

"If you're talking about Granger, I already met him," she says.

"When?" John puts down his coffee mug a little too hard, rattling the plates.

"Late last night. Calling him a character is like saying Cujo was a dog with an attitude problem."

"What did he say to you?" John asks. The laugh lines at the corners of his eyes are gone, replaced by lines on his forehead, a mix of concern and anger.

"It wasn't a big deal," she says. "Besides, I can handle myself. I don't know if you think I need some big strong guy to come riding in to save me or something, but I don't."

"That's not what I..." John takes a deep, steadying breath. "I'm sorry, it's just that Granger's kind of a wild card. You're never quite sure what you're going to get. I should have warned you about him yesterday. I'm sorry."

"I forgive you," she says, picking up her last piece of toast and munching on it. God, she could have eaten an entire second breakfast if it was put in front of her. She looks past John and out over the lake that seduces her senses with its easy grandeur and effortless beauty. When she shifts her attention back to John she sees that his eyes are welled with tears.

"Are you all right?" she asks.

He stands up, grabbing both of their plates and clearing his throat. "So, you're going to be all right here? You feel good about this place?"

She feels like there's a question within the question, but it's a slippery thing, one second in her hands and the next right through her fingers and gone like smoke. He stands, plates in hand, waiting for her answer.

She looks back over the lake, the trees on fire with their changing colors. Then her eyes drift over to the only break in the trees on the far bank. Her eyes aren't as good as they once were, but her visibility is strangely sharp for the distance. Clear as day, she sees the only other cabin on the lake and Granger sitting in a lawn chair at the edge of the water, legs stretched out in front of him and propped up on a dead tree stump. He could pass as just an old man passing time except for the rifle laid across his lap and the binoculars up to his face, staring in her direction. She thinks for a second that he must be looking at something else, that it's just the distance and her own paranoia that makes her think he's staring at her. But then

31

the asshole raises his hand and gives her a little wave, removing all doubt.

"I've always imagined a place like this, a little cabin on a lake to just get away from the world for a while. And in my head, it looked just like this." She nods over to Granger's cabin. "But I admit an old-timer Peeping Tom was never part of the mental image."

John turns to where she's looking and scans the far shore. She can tell he's not picking Granger out. Probably needs glasses and too proud to admit it.

"Granger has his own way about him, to be sure," he says, his back still to her. "Jury's still out on whether that's a good thing or a bad thing." When he turns back to her, his expression is so serious that she involuntarily sits up straighter on the bench, a splinter stabbing painfully through her jeans. "I probably shouldn't say this, but I'm going to anyway. When he tries to tell you something, just be careful. It won't always be the truth."

The words make her throat constrict. It's the same thing Granger said about the cabin. She thought it was a strange thing to say then and she thinks it's strange that John would use exactly the same words. But, as a purveyor of fine words, she doesn't mark these as particularly unique, not so much that it's out of the realm of possibility the two men just stumbled upon the same turn of phrase. It occurs to her she's spent a bit of effort over breakfast explaining away the coincidences.

It's put her on edge and she can't put her finger on why.

"But if you want, there's a pretty easy way to get rid of him," John says, the mischievous look back in his eye.

"How's that?"

"Strut around here in the nude and the old geezer would have a heart attack."

She laughs and it feels good to break the built up tension. John, looking pleased with himself, disappears into the cabin, taking the remains of their breakfast with him. By the time she turns her attention back to Granger, he's gone.

"And no nudity required," she says to the empty world.

CHAPTER 5

John's been gone for a couple of hours and the pages are still blank. Rather than force it, God knows that doesn't work, Rachel grabs her backpack, a small number better suited for schoolbooks than the bottle of Jack she throws into it. She adds a Moleskine notebook and two pens to the mix. Just in case. She's ever the optimist.

Which is why she leaves the gun behind.

The day can't be any more beautiful. Giant puffed clouds drift overhead against a bluebird sky. The sun's warm but not hot, not even when it peeks out from behind the clouds and sends its radiation crashing into her skin at one hundred and eighty-six thousand miles a second. All that speed and energy and all she feels from the collision is a gentle deep warmth and a peaceful sense that regardless of what the human race throws at her, nature means her well.

Walking trails lead in all directions from her new home and she picks one without much thought. *On a whim, out on a limb,* as she remembers someone saying to her when she was young. She supposes it must have been her parents. Or maybe her grandparents as it has the ring of a saying from a different age. But her parents were part of a disappeared age too. Long dead and gone, ghosts from a different time when they might have said things like *On a whim, out on a limb* and thought themselves clever and funny to have such a saying.

She's already well into the woods before she realizes she's wandering so deep in the maze of her own head that she hasn't been paying attention to her surroundings. She stops, takes a breath and gets her bearings. The path behind her is the same as what's ahead. So identical that she has a flash to the road that brought her to the cabin to begin with, long, straight and seeming to go on forever.

She sees a beautiful thing up ahead of her. A doe walks out from a wall of tall ferns, not tentative as deer in her experience tend to be, but brave and clearly unafraid. Rachel holds her breath, afraid that her slightest movement might make the animal dart away.

The deer glances at her, only for a second, and then turns away as if Rachel were no more than another tree in the woods. The doe lowers her muzzle to the ground and eats. Soon, a fawn steps from the protective shield of the ferns. The little guy is not as self-assured as his mother and he takes short, hesitant steps into the open. The youngster knows Rachel is not part of the woods; that she's not just another tree mutely bending to the soft breeze. Rachel is different, foreign. She realizes the doe knows the same thing. She knows the human is an intruder, but she'd deemed her as not a threat to her or her baby. For this, Rachel feels a swell of gratitude. And then a pang of fear. There are humans who would betray this trust and she knows in a rush of insight that the doe's putting herself and her baby in danger.

"Shhaa!" she cries out, thinking there really isn't a typical sound used for shooing away a deer, but *shhaa!* seems like it ought to do the trick. Only the fawn doesn't run, it just looks at her with even greater curiosity. The doe keeps eating.

"Shhaa!" she shouts, waving her arms in the air for good measure. Finally, the doe looks up, munching a mouthful of grass. Not worried. Not a care in the world. Then she walks on, not because she fears anything, but because it is time to continue her walk, her little one in tow.

Rachel watches them go until the fawn disappears into the thick foliage of the forest. A sense of dread grips her and she thinks she might chase after the doe, to scare her, show her that humans can't be trusted, most of all around her baby. But before she can run after them, she hears a new sound that changes her mind.

There's a voice, carried on the wind as delicately as a spiderweb. One second there and then gone, coming and going at the impulse of the breeze. She listens close; it's a song she knows all too well.

"Amazing grace. How sweet the sound..."
She walks toward it, deeper into the forest.
"That saved a wretch like me..."

She's careful. No telling who might be in the wood. Singing the gospels didn't make a man either trustworthy or good. Ten thousand kids knew that story from their childhood, lives wrecked by men who know all the gospels by heart.

"I once was lost, but now I'm found.
Was blind but now I see."

The voice is stronger now, overpowering the breeze that swirls and tries to send the melody in the other direction. It's a man's voice, that much was clear from the beginning. It's deep and hoarse, a soulful voice filled with pain and hurt that only real loss can bring. She's caught by the voice, like its owner is the pied piper from a fairy tale. For the third time in the last day, she tears up, hating her fragility at the same time as she allows the voice to sink into her.

"When we've been here ten thousand years,
Bright shining as the sun,
We've no less days to sing God's praise

Than when we'd first begun."

The man steps into view and the image is so odd that it stops her tears. He's a large man and his enormous body, all three hundred pounds plus of him by her estimation fills out every nook and cranny of his blue jean overalls. He wears brown leather work boots and a baseball cap, the kind with the plastic mesh on the panels except for the front.

But the thing that stopped her tears mid-stream is what the man is doing. Slowly, but with immutable certainty and following the cadence of the hymnal pouring out of him as if he were performing for the Pope himself, the man brandishes a broom back and forth across the forest trail, scattering a mini-tornado of dried leaves and dust with every pass.

He stands in the middle of a large clearing although the canopy of trees still extends overhead. A single shaft of light shines through like a spotlight on a stage. She wonders if that's why the man chose to stand in that exact spot and the sweeping is just part of some show that he's rehearsing.

But she sees that the path that leads from where she stands all the way throughout the clearing is swept perfectly clean, not a single leaf remains.

"I can see you there, miss," the man says. His voice still sounds like sunshine. No, the rumble of water over boulders in a river. "I won't hurt you. I promise."

There's a childlike simplicity in the man's face and the barest touch of something slowed in his speech. Her heart immediately trusts the big man, but her head withholds judgment. She timidly steps out into the clearing.

"My name's Oliver Leonard Peterson," he says, sounding each word out carefully, reminding her of a grade school student reciting his name to a teacher. He snatches his hat from his head like he's been caught wearing it inside a church and clutches it to his chest. "But people usually just call me Ollie. You know, like the game?" He suddenly calls out, "Ollie Ollie oxen free." He tilts his head to a side, sizing up her reaction. When she smiles at him, he returns it and looks relieved. "What's your name, miss?"

"Rachel," she answers, walking toward him. She scans the forest on either side to see if there are other men there. Ones that don't sing like angels.

"Just me out here," Ollie says, picking up on the fact that her head is on a swivel. "Well, me and my best girl here," he says, lifting up his broom toward her. "But she's never hurt no-one. Except to give me a few blisters every now and then, I guess."

She smiles and feels guilty for being suspicious. "Sorry, just didn't expect to come across anyone out here is all."

"You and me both," Ollie says. "Don't see a lot of people when I'm working. At least any that stop to talk anyway." He pulls his hat on and his posture relaxes. He leans forward and whispers, "Between me and you, I'm just glad I got my shirt on. Gets hot after awhile working, so sometimes I take it off. Momma's always telling me, *No one wants to see you with your shirt off so you leave it on, Ollie.*" He chuckles at his own expense, and the sound is soothing, like far-away thunder. "I suppose she's right about that."

She laughs with him, her brain catching up with her heart that Ollie Peterson isn't a threat. Maybe odd, but no threat.

Ollie curbs his laughter but the joy stays in his eyes. She isn't sure how long he's been at work in the forest, or why, but he seems to be enjoying the break.

"I don't know anything about your shirt, off or on," she says, trying to match his warmth, "but you have a voice. Man, do you ever."

"Geez," Ollie says, taking a swipe at a leaf near his feet. "I don't know about that. Now Momma, she had what my Aunt Vie called a carryin' voice. Carried right up to Heaven itself. I can't sing anything like that."

"Your voice is beautiful," she says. "And it carries just fine."

Ollie looks embarrassed by the compliment and swipes the air with his hand as if to push it away. Still, he looks pleased by it. "You visiting or staying for good?" he asks.

"Visiting," she says. The second she says it she wonders where she plans on going when she leaves. She doesn't have a good answer.

"You don't look too sure about that," Ollie says. "Don't worry, lots of people aren't sure when they first get here. But they figure it out."

"Figure what out?"

"If they need to stay or not." He looks around the forest, leaning on his broom. "Worse places to be, I suppose."

She slides the backpack off and lets it fall to the ground. Bending down, she unzips it and pulls out the bottle of Jack, then twists off the cap. She has Ollie's full attention.

"Want some?" she asks, holding the bottle out.

It's Ollie's turn to check the forest around them. "That's not really allowed," he says, but his hand is already outstretched toward her. "But don't want to be rude, seeing as how we just met."

"Neighborly of you," she says, assuming a man sweeping the woods with a broom must live close by. She hands over the bottle and watches as he takes a swig. His eyes open wide in surprise at the taste, but he takes a heavy pull before handing it back. She does the same. They're likely family now, she and Ollie, this strange man whose mom bestowed on him a voice able to make the angels weep. They're family and family shares stories, so she decides to ask for his.

"Can I ask you something, Ollie?"

"Sure, miss," he says. "Anything you want."

She nods at the broom. "I appreciate a man who likes to clean up, lord knows that's a rarity. But what's the point?"

"How do you mean?" Ollie says, his eyebrows puckering together in a confused look.

"You're standing in the middle of the forest. Sweeping leaves. There's never an end. It's pointless."

Ollie looks around him and she feels terrible for what she's said. The man's eyes turn sad, like a light's gone out, and she feels responsible.

"Miss, I've been cleaning up long as I've been able. I clean up after adults, after kids, after dogs, or even after thousands of trees shedding their leaves. You clean because it's a job. But even when it stops being a job, you clean because for just a little while, the world's better for it."

She should leave it at that. But she doesn't, because she can't.

"But it's... it's..."

"Futile?" Ollie offers up.

Rachel nods. It's the perfect word and she chastises herself for being surprised he comes up with it. There was clearly more to Ollie than met the eye. "Yes, isn't it futile?"

"Momma used to tell me stories when I was growing up on account we didn't have a TV and the radio hardly ever worked. Her favorites were the Bible stories, of course. But she was pretty charged up by the Greeks too. Ever heard the Greek stories with all their gods and heroes and creatures?"

She's more than heard the stories. She's written dozens of papers about Greek and Roman mythology. She's read them in the original Greek and defended a thesis on Dante's use of ancient mythologies in his fourteenth century epic poem, *Divine Comedy*. All of this rattles off in her mind even though she can't recall clearly where she was a week ago.

"Have you heard any of 'em?" Ollie asks again.

She nods. "A few of them."

"My favorite was about Sisyphus, you know that one?"

She does but she wants to hear his version. "I heard it a long time ago but I'd love to hear you tell it."

"The way Momma told it was that there was this Greek king who angered the gods. She never did tell us what the man did, but it had to be bad because the gods sure were pissed off at the poor guy." A horrified look appears on his face. "Pardon my French," he says.

"French all you want," she says and gets a smile from the big man.

"So Sisyphus dies and finds himself at the bottom of this big mountain, and he's got a big round rock at his feet. Zeus, he's the main god, tells him that to get into Paradise he only has got to do one thing. Roll that rock up to the top of the mountain. So Sisyphus rolls up his sleeves and gets to work. The rock is heavy, real heavy, but he's a strong fellah and he has time. He strains. He pushes. His arms and legs get all scratched up and bloody, but he's making progress higher and higher up the mountain. Then, just as he's about dead on his feet, exhausted, beaten down, he sees that he's almost to the top. He gets all excited. The power in his muscles comes back and he heaves that stone up. He's almost there when the worst possible thing happens." Ollie pauses for effect and it works. She knows the story but she still leans forward, waiting. "That rock slips away, gets past him and down the mountain. It rolls and rolls and rolls down the hill, all the way to the exact spot where he started.

"Sisyphus is mad. But he just walks down the mountain, stretches out his muscles and... can you guess what he does?"

"Starts again."

"Right," Ollie says, eyes on fire like he's the Greek king looking up to the top of the mountain. The slow, mumbling speech pattern he'd had when she'd first met him is long gone. He's on a roll. "Sisyphus just leans his back into that rock and he heaves it up the mountain. This time it's twice as hard cause his muscles are sore, his arms are all chewed up, he's bleeding from cuts all over. But, he pushes on. Up the mountain. To the top. To the promise of recompense and forgiveness, salvation and eternal paradise."

The words roll off his tongue so easily that they sound like he's quoting from memory, maybe a hymn or a recent sermon. She thinks Ollie has missed his calling as a preacher. He could have been a real Bible-thumper, filling tents nightly on weekdays and three times on the weekends. If he hadn't been so busy sweeping leaves in the forest, that is.

"But when he gets near the top," Ollie's voice is low now, almost a whisper, like it's just the two of them in the whole wide world that will know the story and how it ends. "Just as he's gonna get it over the top, BAM!" He claps his massive hands together and the sound literally echoes through the forest and she jumps back. "That rock rolls back down the mountain, through the bushes and the trees and the rocks. All the way down to the exact spot where he started." Ollie pauses here and takes stock of his audience of one. Rachel thinks she must have the right expression he's looking for because he smiles wide.

"Sisyphus may have been a sinner. He may have done some bad doo-doo to make the gods so angry. But one thing is for sure, he's not stupid. He sees that the rock has come to rest in the exact same place not once, but twice in a row. And he knows the terrible thing."

"That the gods aren't ever going to let him win," she whispers.

Ollie moves his hands through the air like he's a magician who just made a rabbit appear out of thin air. "It's futile," he says, loading the word with all the gravitas of his deep baritone delivery. "Totally and utterly futile."

"Like sweeping the leaves off a hiking trail in autumn," she says as if he's the one missing the point of his own story.

45

But Ollie wags his finger like she's been a particularly bad student. "Sisyphus knows what's going on. He knows he can't win, so you know what he does? He lowers his shoulder into the rock and heads to the top of the mountain. It rolls down again and he starts again. Fails. Tries again. Fails. Tries again. Fails. Tries again."

"Why?"

"Don't you see? It's because that's the last part of him that's still alive," Ollie says. "No matter the chance of him making it, no matter if the gods are all lined up against him, trying is all he's got. It's all any of us has got. That's that makes us human. We just keep on going no matter what's thrown at us. Picking our way through. Finding a way to keep breathing one day after the other. Even when it's futile." Ollie clutches his broom with both hands. "And the minute any of us give that up, then we're just lost forever, aren't we?"

She feels like Ollie expects something from her. Applause? Tears? An answer? An *Oh my God* moment where she admits sweeping leaves in the forest is a noble cause? She can't do any of those things so she stares at him.

He kicks the leaves at his feet. When he talks, his speech has slowed again and he mumbled his words. "Sorry, didn't mean to get on my soapbox or nothing. Momma says I run my mouth too much sometimes."

"No," she says. "It was a fine story. I'm glad you told it. Really, I am."

An awkward silence stretches out between them.

"So?" he finally asks. "What d'ya think of all that?"

She laughs. "Ollie, I think this is the oddest couple of days I've ever had. For a place that's supposed to be isolated I've had a run of interesting conversations recently. My landlord is an odd duck. There's that freak show Granger from across the lake. And now—"

"You've been meeting with Granger?" Ollie says, his eyes wide, almost bulging. "Why didn't you tell me that?"

She takes a step back, not liking his tone. "What's the big deal?"

Ollie steps toward her. His bulky body seems larger close up, more muscular than she realized. She has a flash of insight that if she screams, he could snap her neck like it was no more than a chicken bone if he wanted. Maybe doing it by accident from trying to quiet her because he doesn't know his own strength.

"You never saw me, you understand?" Ollie says, his voice dark and menacing. "And don't you dare ever say we talked."

She backs up, ready to run if she needs to. Then something occurs to her and she stops her retreat.

"You're scared of him," she says. "Of Granger. Why? He's just an old man."

Ollie's face loses all the anger and intimidation he tried to direct at her. He softens and the angel with the carryin' voice is back.

"I'm so sorry, miss," he says, looking like he might cry. "Didn't mean to raise my voice. I should've never stopped working. Should've kept to myself like I'm supposed to. I hope things work out for you. I really do. Just please don't mention my name."

"I won't," she says. "I promise."

His face looks so thankful when she agrees to keep the secret that she can't bring herself to use it as leverage to get more information out of him.

"I won't tell him regardless," she says. "But will you tell me why you're so scared of him?"

Ollie shakes his head. Somehow, even with all of his size he looks like a kid standing there, twisting the broom handle with his hands. "I can't tell you that. It's just not the way things work around here."

"Ollie, what the hell are you talking about?"

Ollie turns his back to her and sweeps the path. Slow, deliberate strokes of his broom. He mutters over and over, "It's just not how things work around here. It's just not how things work around here."

Chapter 6

Rachel wakes just as the sun begins to set behind the mountains on the far side of the lake. She's up with a start, a disoriented jump from the darkness of sleep into the flesh and blood reality of the world. There's a panicked gasp of air as she pushes away a heavy weight smothering her.

But there's nothing there. Only a faint echo of a dream that she senses was brilliant Technicolor only seconds earlier, but now disintegrates wherever she tries to grasp it. All that's left of the dream is the smell of the world burning, lingering strongly enough that she searches the room for signs of smoke, thinking her

49

dream world had stolen the idea from the real. But there is nothing. Only the couch where she napped, the dining table where Underwood smirks at her, still unused, and the kitchen, as equally ignored as the typewriter. No smoke. No fire. It's no matter because all thoughts of either drift away with the rest of her forgotten dream and she lets it happen. There's no fight in her to remember. She didn't come to the cabin to remember, anyway.

She stands and stretches, shocked by how long she's slept. There's no clock or watch in the house or on her person, one of her writing retreat rules, but the light outside tells her the story. As the final bit of sun ducks behind the mountain in that curious sped up way typical of the last seconds of the sunset, she has a foreboding sense that time is somehow moving faster than it should. But that's crazy, just her imagination taking advantage of her blurry state of mind.

That's jus' not how things work around here.

It's Ollie's voice in her head, but somehow she knows he's right. Time doesn't move faster here. It's not how things work.

Thinking of work, she walks over to the dining room table and is surprised to see a piece of paper rolled into Underwood's gleaming paper feeder, the metal bar snug against it, ready for business.

"You hoping to get lucky tonight, big guy?" she says. She waits, half-expecting the keys to thump out an answer to her question. But they don't. They haven't for a long time. "Let me use the bathroom first," she says. "Help yourself to a drink."

She turns to the sliding door to go outside but stops herself, surprised to find she means to pee outside. She's embarrassed by the idea even though there's no one else there. "Get a grip," she mumbles, walking through the cabin and using the bathroom like a normal person. When she's done, she pours herself a drink from the bottle in the kitchen, then returns to the table to face her tormentor.

Fingers on the keys. White page ready for her brilliance. Begging for it. And she wants to give it. More than that, she wants to stuff it down Underwood's throat so hard he gags on it.

Her fingers move, slow at first, tentative. Then faster, speed building and building, until she's dancing over the keys. The metal prongs, each with its own letter, smack through the black ink ribbon and stamp the paper. Her left hand swats the return register without being told when it's time to do so. This is it, the old magic. She closes her eyes, swaying to the musicality of the words in her head, relishing the sense of them traveling through her nervous system in electrical impulses telling her hands what to do. Loving that all of it, this dance, this kinetic energy, this alchemy of creation, is thoughts made real. All she has to do to see inside her own mind is open her eyes, look at the page and see...

...a half-page of neat typing. First line indented. Hyphenated words at right margin. Two paragraph breaks. Lines of dialogue in quotes. And not a single actual word that makes sense.

Gibberish.

All of it.

She rocks back in her chair. The slew of jumbled consonants and vowels blur from the tears in her eyes. She closes her hands into fists, not wanting to see the fingers that betrayed her trust. At that moment, bursting through the veil that's dropped down over her mind, comes the image of a man typing at a desk. She knows the place in this image, it's called the Overlook Hotel and she'd been there many times. The man looks up as if she's standing in the room with him and points to the manuscript on his desk. She already knows what's there but looks anyway. Page after page of the phrase, *All work and no play makes Jack a dull boy.* The man rips the page from this typewriter and shakes it at her. "You can't even form a goddamn word?" he yells, crushes the paper in his hand and throws it at her. "What the fuck is wrong with you?"

BAM

A sound shakes the image from her head. The angry man and his piece of paper are gone.

BAM

BAM

Something at the door. The one between the living room and the kitchen. She only uses the sliding door on the deck to come and go, but this door faces the road. It's dark and she doesn't expect anyone. A wave of terror passes through her as she immediately thinks of every murder and torture scene she's ever written or considered writing.

BAM

The door shakes with each hit. The top half of it is glass, separated into four panes. She draws a sharp breath when she sees movement through the window. But she can't make out what it is. Maybe the wolves she heard last night? But wolves didn't use doors, did they?

If it's someone knocking, they're using a forearm or their foot. Or knuckles they didn't mind pummeling into a bloody mess.

BAM

She has a panicked moment thinking that it's the man from the Overlook Hotel, but she remembers that's impossible. The man is from someone else's mind. He's someone else's responsibility.

BAM

One of the squares of glass breaks and this wakes her up from her frozen state. She grabs the gun on the table next to Underwood, not even having realized it was there. Over to the kitchen, doing her best not to be seen by whoever is outside the door.

BAM

Now that she's closer, she can see that there's a single trail of blood dripping down the inside of the door from where the glass is broken. Her breath comes in short, ragged pants and she can't control her shaking hands. She steals a look outside and sees a black shape fly at the door.

BAM

She lets out a short scream as more glass breaks. Something *flutters* outside. She reaches out to the wall and flips a switch to turn on the light outside. It doesn't work. The door shakes again from another collision.

BAM.

She flips the switch up and down. Still dark. Of course it is. The generator's not on.

The second this thought crosses her mind, the light outside flickers on, then flares so bright that she has to shy away from it.

Through squinted eyes, she turns back to see that the glass is smeared with blood and black feathers.

She opens the door even though she really doesn't want to. On the small landing is a massive bird. She can only see its body but its hulking mass reminds her of a turkey vulture, the carrion eater always cleaning up the deer carcasses on the side of roads. But there's something different about this one. Its black feathers look oily in the light from the porch's single light bulb, but also mottled, holes eaten through, covered in dirt and cobwebs. One wing is bent backward, clearly broken, even a white flash of bone sticking out as it thrashes on the ground.

Then she sees the head.

Featherless. Raw flesh oozing blood. Two oversized eye sockets, one empty with a festering sore. The other a maniac's eye, rolling around, unable to stop itself. The mouth isn't a bird's. It's human. With cracked, blistered lips that are pressed together and sewn shut with leather string.

Impossibly, the bird pushes itself off the ground with wiry legs, flaps its one good wing even as the broken one grinds on the exposed bone. It launches itself at her and she screams. With a swing of her arm, she bats the thing away. The gun's in her hand and smashes into the oozing head, knocking the bird sideways. It hits the ground again, a mewling cry coming from behind its sutured mouth.

The bird gets back up and cocks its head toward her. That rolling eye comes to rest, locked on her. As she watches, the eye fills with blood, a dribble of it leaking from a puncture in the bottom so that it cries black tears. She sees the bird's talons, thick and sharp. They clack against the wood of the deck and she has no problem imagining them sunk deep into her flesh.

The bird lunges. Her hand jerks up and she puts a bullet into its skull right through the one good eye. The back of the bird's head blows out and the faded paint on the entryway's railing splatters black. The bird slumps to the ground. Not moving.

She's breathing hard, like she'd run a race. The gun feels heavy in her hand and the nose lowers to the ground as she stares at the bird lying in the expanding pool of blood. Not a turkey vulture. Not some prehistoric monster after all.

Just a common black raven with a broken wing.

And now with half its head shot off.

A howl erupts from the forest down closer to the water. Close enough that she jumps at the sound and swings the gun that direction, her hand shaking. There are shadows in the tree line. Five or six from what she can tell. Dark shapes that weave in and out of the trees. She thinks she sees glowing eyes, but she's not sure. The howls come altogether this time, layering on top of one another until they harmonize into one wistful, terrible note.

Slowly, she backs into the cabin, the gun swinging back and forth in front of her. She closes the door and locks it. Then she pulls the thin curtain shut across the window as if that could keep out the things after her.

Because they are after her.

Somehow she knows this as clearly as she knows her own name. They mean to get her and devour her. They mean to destroy her once and for all.

The howls come again, so loud that she can't believe they're not already somewhere inside the house. She backs into the main room, cursing the sliding glass doors that cover the far wall and leave her so exposed. But the attack doesn't come from the sliding glass door. When it comes, it's from the window right in front of her.

The glass explodes like a bomb's gone off. She shields her face with her arms but she still feels the sting of the glass shards slicing into her skin. Even so, she risks watching what's coming through the window. She can't stop herself from seeing it for herself, this thing that's tracked her down.

It's a wolf, this she already knew. But it's enormous, its head as high as her own. Black mangy fur hangs in matted tufts. Open wounds cover its body, seeping with infection. The thing smells like rotten meat, a sharp rancidity that makes her gag. The wolf snarls, baring black teeth. Its eyes glow with hate and knowing.

She holds up the gun and screams at the beast. "Leave me alone!"

The wolf leaps at her. She fires the gun and the window shatters behind the creature.

Still, the blast from the gun gets the beast's attention and makes it twist in midair to miss her. It knocks into the table, sending Underwood and the paper flying. The wolf scrambles to find its balance. If she has her way, it never will.

She pulls the trigger as fast as she can, the blasts from the gun drowning out her screams.

But the wolf is quick, more nimble than she expected, and is back on its feet. It doesn't react to the bullets she knows must be hitting it. She thinks it will take a run at her and it will all be over, but instead it jumps over the couch and bounds out of the cabin through the window.

It takes her several seconds before she realizes she's still pulling the trigger on the empty gun.

Click. Click. Click.

Aiming at where she imagines the wolf waits for her out in the night.

In time, the howls rise again, but they are farther away now. And retreating.

She breaks down and sobs, the gun dropping to the floor, useless anyway. She holds her arms across her stomach and rocks back and forth. But not for long. On the floor in front of her is a single dime-sized point of light. None of her lanterns in the cabin shine like that.

Looking up, she draws in a sharp breath. The far wall of the cabin, right where she shot repeatedly at the wolf, there are more than a dozen beams of light projected out from bullet-sized holes in the wall.

She picks up a piece of crumpled typing paper from the floor next to her, one that used to be part of the taunting stack next to Underwood. She pushes it along the floor toward the point of light in front of her until the circle hits the edge of the paper.

Nothing happens.

She laughs and it sounds strange to her ears. She thought it was going to burst into flames or something, but it didn't. It's just light. But from where?

Standing up, she walks across the room, the shafts of light playing across her body. She knows what she has to do next, but she doesn't want to do it. Even though the howls are gone, she can't be sure the wolf isn't right outside waiting to attack. She grabs the gun from the floor, pokes her head through the sliding door and looks back and forth. Seeing nothing, she risks a quick run to the end of the deck and leans out, seeing the entire length of the cabin that makes up the wall emitting the light.

Nothing but darkness.

She runs back inside, not wanting to stay outside a minute longer than she needs. The beams of light are still there, like taut strings stretched across the room. And there's something she didn't notice before. One of the bullets near the bottom did more than just punch a hole in the wall, it ripped away a section the size of a fist. Light pours through this gap, but there's something more. There's movement on the other side. Hardly perceptible, just a flicker in the light.

She darts across the room, staying on one side of the hole and gets on her knees. Her entire body trembles and she clutches herself trying to get under control. It's no use. She feels the anxiety building. It pounds inside her head, ratcheting up until she whimpers. Still, she forces herself to slide forward, her shoulder brushing against the wall as she does. The gun is still in her hand and she thinks about reloading before looking through the hole. She decides against it. There's no way she wants to leave the wall she's pressed against. She's not sure if she wants to look in the hole at all. Her gut tells her she shouldn't. Or, at the very least, that she's not meant to.

Nothing good will come of it.

She closes her eyes and sucks in a deep, shuddering breath. *On a whim, out on a limb.* When she opens them, she's made her decision to look. She's going to find out what's there.

She leans forward, inch-by-inch, her left cheek pressed against the wall, ready to see, ready to know.

Then flames lick out from the hole in the wall and she hears the crackle and hiss of a fire. The sight and sound sends her to the floor on all fours, a sudden pain stabbing through her chest. God it hurts. She's going to die right there on the cabin floor. The flames shoot through the other holes in the wall. Soon the whole place will be an inferno. Even at this thought, she can't move. Can't breathe. It feels like there's something sitting on her chest.

Even with this weight, and even with the pain, she manages to scream.

Then white hot pain explodes in the back of her neck and races down her spine. She falls to the floor and rolls over on her back. As she does, Granger comes into full view, eyes wild, lips parted in a snarl, a frying pan held over his head.

"For your own good," he says.

"No," she manages as the frying pan begins its descent.

This time there's no pain. Only darkness. And silence.

CHAPTER 7

"Is she going to be all right?"

"How do you mean?"

"You know damn well what I mean."

"Anger is not welcome here. In fact, one might say it is counterproductive."

"I'm not angry."

"You seem angry."

"No... I... I didn't mean it that way."

Pause.

"You are concerned."

"Of course I am. Aren't you?"

"The question is naïve."

"How long will it be?"

"That is difficult to say. An hour? An afternoon? A day?"

"A week?"

"I doubt it. The important thing is that she was discovered in time."

Pause.

"Would you not agree?"

"Yes, of course."

Pause.

"This is hard for you. I understand."

"You have no concept of how hard this is for me, so don't even imply that you do, you smug bastard."

Pause.

"I'm sorry. It's just... it's been... you know."

"Wait outside please. I will have you brought to me if you're needed."

"But..."

"That is not a request."

"When she wakes up, tell her... tell her..."

"Tell her what?"

"Tell her nothing."

CHAPTER 8

The air burns. Acrid and greasy.

She's in a car but gravity is upside down. Her seatbelt cinches into her neck and chest, holding all of her body weight. There's pressure all over her face, something suffocating her. She pushes against it and it gives way. Soon she can see what it is. A white bag, smooth as silk, deflates in front of her, falling to the ceiling as it does. The windshield is broken and smoke pours into the car. Her mouth tastes salty and metallic. She wipes it with her hand, which comes back covered with blood. There's a flash of light in front of her and a rush of heat.

She cries out and sits up. She's in bed, drenched with sweat, heart pounding in her chest. The second she's up, she regrets it. Blood surges to her head, punishing her with a headache so intense she has to grab the mattress on either side of her, twisting the sheets in a white-knuckled grip. The greasy burning smell from her dream is real enough and the stench of it in the cabin turns her stomach. Tentatively, she reaches up to feel her head, certain she's going to find a machete buried in her skull the way she feels. There's no machete though, just a tender area on the side of her head.

Granger.

It comes back to her in a flood and the nausea rushes back with it. She remembers everything from the night before, ending with the image of Granger and his frying pan.

A voice wafts through the air, intertwined with the burning smell. The voice is singing but it's rough and graveled, slightly off-key. She knows the voice. Granger's still in the house.

She looks around the room for a weapon. The bedroom is sparse, just a bed, a nightstand with a lamp and a chest of drawers. She stands and the world spins, nearly throwing her back down to the bed. But she knows she's in danger so the adrenaline helps clear her head.

The singing is clearer now. Or maybe Granger is louder, she can't be sure. She picks up pieces of the song. *Amazing Grace*, just like Ollie singing in the woods, but it's a verse she doesn't recognize.

"Yea, when this flesh and hear shall fail,
And mortal life shall cease..."

Granger's singing is discordant and off-key, almost as if he were mocking the idea of the song.

"I shall possess, within the veil,
A life of joy and peace..."

She opens the small closet, still desperate for a weapon. With some effort, she knocks loose the wood rod meant for hanging clothes. It's nice and heavy, not one of those cheap jobs. She grips it with both hands like a baseball bat. It's not much as far as weapons go, but it will have to do.

She opens the door and the burning smell hits her like a wall. The short hallway leading to the kitchen and the main room is hazy with blue smoke. She holds onto the wall for balance and walks toward the kitchen, trying her best to steady her breathing.

Granger stands over the counter, next to the stove, his back to her, still humming the song. There are two skillets on the stove that billow with foul smoke. Granger's elbow works up and down in a scissoring motion, then he turns and dumps a handful of chopped onions into the skillet. The grease sizzles and a new cloud of smoke rises up in the room.

She grips the wood pole in her hand and imagines herself beaning the old man in the back of the head, his old bones shattering from the impact. She steels herself for action, confident that she has the element of surprise on her side. There's no way the man knows she's behind him.

"Good morning," Granger says without bothering to turn around, dispelling that idea. "There're three aspirin on the table for you." He points to the front room with the carving knife in his hand. It's long and serrated, better suited for field dressing large game than dicing vegetables. "Breakfast will be ready in a few minutes."

She shakes her head, trying to clear the fog from it. None of this makes sense.

"I know what you did," she says, surprised at how hoarse her voice sounds. "I saw you."

Granger turns. His hair is combed back and he's wearing a flannel shirt with an apron tied around his waist. He looks genuinely surprised to see that she's holding the wood pole in her hands. It's not lost on her that he shifts his grip on his knife, the kitchen tool turning into a weapon.

"And I saw you," Granger says. "And now here we are."

"You hit me."

"You can thank me for that later."

Flames flare up in one of the skillets and Granger turns back to his cooking like he's Debbie homemaker. "Hope you like your breakfast meats. I've got enough for a small army here."

"What are you..." her voice trails off. In the main room, she spots the table set up with Underwood in the center and a small pile of blank paper next to it. She walks toward it, ignoring Granger.

The room is bathed in morning sun and it reminds her of the light coming from the bullet holes in the wall. She steps over to the wall and runs her hand across it. Perfectly smooth. Not a single hole in it.

"Looking for something?" Granger asks from behind her.

She shakes her head. "There were... holes in the wall last night." She points to the broken window on the other side of the room, feeling a sense of relief. "A wolf. A black wolf jumped through that window."

Granger walks over and inspects the area. "A wolf, huh? Window's broken all right," he says. "But all the glass is outside. I'm no detective, but I'd say that means it was broken from in here."

She joins him, wood pole still in her hands, but dragging behind her now. He's right, there isn't a single sliver of glass on the floor.

"You can try the wolf story on the guy you rented the place from if you're worried about a deposit or something. Not sure if he's goin' to buy it," Granger says. "Oh, this is yours." He pulls her gun from the front apron pocket and tosses it to her. "Not loaded, of course. Not after last night."

She catches the gun and looks puzzled.

"You know," Granger says. He shapes his fingers into a gun like he's a kid playing cops and robbers. He sticks out his lower lip and pretends to be crying as he holds the end of his finger gun to his head, then opens his mouth and inserts it there. Then he grins and lowers his hand. "Like I said, you can thank me later for knockin' you aside the head. Good thing I came over when I did before you hit anything you were aiming for. Besides, the way you were ramping up, I thought your head was about to explode. You were pretty upset about something." He waits and she can't do much more than stare at him blankly. "I guess the thank you will have to wait," he finally says. "Go on. Sit on the deck, I'll bring breakfast."

Granger doesn't wait for an answer, but goes back to the kitchen, humming a new gospel song she doesn't recognize. She almost goes outside as he suggested, but swings by the table first and leans over to look at the paper set up in Underwood.

She remembers the writing session from the night before, the feeling like it was back and flowing again, only to open her eyes and see nonsense on the page.

Now there's only one sentence typed on the page. And she doesn't even need to look at it to know what it says, but she can't help but read it.

All work and no play makes Jack a dull boy.

CHAPTER 9

"Hope you're hungry," Granger says, banging a plate of food down on the table in front of her before taking the seat on the opposite side of the bench.

Her stomach turns over at the sight of it. For all the smoke and the flames, the plate is mostly bloody morsels of meat and undercooked sausage surrounded by charred potatoes. There are fried eggs with soft centers leaking their yolks in slow dribbles. She closes her eyes and sees the black bird's damaged eye with its trickle of blood tears. She hasn't opened the front door yet to look out there, but she did notice there was no broken windowpane, which meant there was a better than good chance there was no bird there either.

"What's a matter?" Granger says, his mouth full, yolk dripping from his lips. "Dig in."

She pushes the plate away and drinks the coffee in front of her. She wants something stronger. Granger notices her look toward the cabin.

"I looked for some to add."

"What?" she says, embarrassed.

"Hair of the dog and all that. You finished off what you had, everything I could find anyway. Maybe that's why... you know." He twirls his finger around the side of his head. "Cuckoo for Cocoa Puffs."

She knows she should be offended, but she can't find the energy. She sips from her mug.

"This coffee is for shit," she says.

Granger laughs, bits of food flying from his mouth. "I knew I was going to like you."

She looks out over the lake. "When I first saw you, you told me that the cabin might try to talk to me. And that if it did, I shouldn't listen because it wouldn't always be the truth."

Granger turns serious, even wiping his greasy lips with the front of his shirt. "Yeah, I said that."

"Something's happening here," she says. "And I think you know what it is."

Granger leans forward and she notices for the first time how intense his eyes are. They're not looking at her. They're looking into her. She feels her skin prickle and fights the urge to wrinkle her nose in disgust. "S'pose I do? S'pose I don't? Think it'll make a difference either way?"

"Any difference to what?"

Granger makes a grand gesture at the world around them. "Everything. That's all there is, am I right? Can I get a hallelujah from the choir?"

She stares until she can't stand the way his eyes look at her any longer. They feel like hands groping her body.

"I guess you're not in the mood," he says, licking his lips suggestively. "More's the pity."

"What's wrong with you?" she says, hating that it only comes out as a whisper.

"Says the girl trying to drink whiskey with a bullet chaser."

"I wasn't going to…"

"You would have," Granger says. "That's as certain as death and the Devil." He winks at her like she's a teenager and he's the captain of the football team. "You can quote me on that."

"I need to get out of here. The things I'm seeing, the wolves, people sweeping the woods, you showing up and—"

Granger whips his head around. "Sweeping in the woods? You saw Ollie, didn't you? When?" The Mr. Nice-Guy pretense is gone. Granger's face twists into a mask of outrage. "Did you talk to him?"

She feels a wave of guilt for bringing up Ollie, especially since she'd specifically promised him she wouldn't. But it hadn't been on purpose

71

and now that it's out there, she finds Granger's reaction interesting. She senses the power shift in her direction and she wonders why. "S'pose I did? S'pose I didn't? Think it'll make a difference either way?"

Granger hits the table with his hand and the plates jump. He stands up. "Tell me. Did you talk to him? What did he say?"

She stands up too, pushing her chair back so hard that it falls over. She leans forward, fists on the table. "Tell me what's going on at this lake. In this cabin. Tell me and I'll tell you what Ollie said."

Granger locks on to her with his intense eyes and this time she doesn't back down. Finally, he grins, projecting all the false confidence of the bully who backs down when his target unexpectedly fights back. "That's more like it," he says. "I was waiting to see if there was some fire in that belly of yours."

She just stares back at him even though all she wants to do is yell at him to tell her what he knows. Worse, she has the impulse to crawl across the table and beat him, to scratch out his eyes with her nails. She doesn't know where the idea comes from and she doesn't like it. "Tell me or get out of here," she says.

"It's jus' not how things work around here," Granger says.

She imagines Ollie sweeping the woods, leaves drifting down around him like snowflakes, a never-ending thankless job.

"Then get out of here," she says. "And leave me alone."

Granger eyeballs her, then hocks up a loogie and spits it on the table in front of her. "To hell with you," he says and then stomps off the deck.

She watches him leave, willing at first to just let him go. But he was right about one thing, there's plenty of fire in her belly now. "Thanks for breakfast," she calls out. "It sucked."

Granger doesn't even turn around, he just holds up his right hand and gives her the finger as he walks away.

She picks up the plates of food, wrinkling her nose at the disgusting concoction sliding around in grease, blood and yolk. She thinks about forking it off into the bushes so it doesn't stink up the house, but she doesn't want to attract any animals, especially the ones that visited her last night. If in fact they had visited her.

Food disposal comes first, tying off a garbage bag and scraping off all of the leftovers and the solidified grease left in the frying pans. She opens the front door to take out the trash, forgetting until she's already outside that the front porch is where the bird carcass is. But there is no bird. Just like there's no missing glass in the window in the door. Or wolves prowling the forest looking for her.

She drops the trash and goes back inside, slamming the door behind her. As she does, the square of the window she thought was broken the night before pops out and shatters on the floor.

"Damn it."

She bends down to pick up the pieces, knowing if she doesn't then one will end up buried in her bare foot at some point. As she picks them up, she notices something odd. Stuck to the edge of the glass is a layer of putty. She peels some of it off and rolls it in her fingers. It has the consistency of Play-Doh, soft and malleable. She stands and taps the glass pane next to the section that popped out, then feels the edges. Hard, cracked with age and weathering. The window that broke the night before is brand new. Someone repaired it while she slept. But why?

She opens the door and kneels down on her hands and knees to inspect the decking of the raised entryway. The wood slats are aged, worn by decades of hard New England seasons. There's dirt rubbed into every crack. A thin layer of moss grows on the far edge where there's no disturbance from foot traffic. But none of this is what she's looking for. She puts her eye right up to the narrow space between the boards and examines the length of it before moving to the next one. And the next. On the third try, she sees something and lets out a little cry of excitement. She has to scramble down the short run of stairs to grab a small twig as a tool, then returns and stabs it into the crack. Twisting it just right, she lifts her find out high enough from the crack to pinch it between her thumb and forefinger. Carefully so as not to tear it, she extracts an eighteen-inch, single black feather from the crack. She holds it up, certain it's from the bird she killed last night. No little raven feather either, but one that looks like it came from the big, ugly son of a bitch she'd first seen.

This was proof. Someone had cleaned up the mess.

Fixed the window.

Removed the bird.

Put the glass from the other window outside.

Granger. It had to be.

But why?

She tosses the feather, goes back inside the cabin and heads straight to the kitchen. One-by-one, she flings open the drawers and rifles through the contents looking for tools. She pulls out a meat tenderizer and puts it on the counter. The same with an oversized salad fork. But when she looks under the kitchen sink, she forgets those options as her hand wraps around the handle of a claw hammer. It couldn't have been a better tool if she'd imagined it herself.

Hammer in hand, she walks across the cabin, not even acknowledging Underwood still squatting in the center of the dinner table. She heads straight for the wall she shot up the night before, rubbing her free hand over the surface. It takes a few seconds, but she comes to a patch that feels different than the rest of the wall. She looks at it closely, then touches her finger to the spot and pushes, sinking her finger in up to her first knuckle into soft putty. It's the bullet hole.

"Son of a bitch," she says to herself. "What the hell are you hiding behind this wall?"

She rears back and smashes the hammer into the wall. It breaks into the drywall, sinking a dent in the surface several inches wide. She swings again, the hammer spinning in her hand so that the claw end sinks in. She yanks on it and a chunk of the wall comes with it, sending a cloud of dust into the air.

With a yell, she hits the wall again. Harder. Ripping through the old crumbling drywall. She slams into it again and again, hardly noticing the rising pile of debris around her feet. She strikes faster, breathing hard, sweat covering her body. She hits the wall until her hands ache and her muscles quiver. Enlarging the hole, working to the edges, knowing in her heart that she's uncovering something vital.

Then, just as suddenly as she started, she's done. She steps back from the wall. The surface is obscured, dust drifting in the filtered sunlight. A breeze moves through the cabin, parting the cloud.

And there it is. A door. Right in the middle of the wall.

Begging to be opened.

She stares at the door, slowly regretting that she went looking for it. She eyes the debris covering the floor and wonders whether it's possible to fit the pieces back together and repair the wall. She spends a few seconds imagining the effort it would take before giving up on the idea.

She walks up to the door and places her hand carefully on its surface. It's cool to the touch, colder than it ought to be. She's surprised to see how deep inside the wall the door is set, maybe a foot or more. Part of her was hoping it was just an old exterior door covered up in a remodel, but she knows that's not the case. She's looked at the cabin from the outside and if this was part of the wall then it would have stuck out from the wood siding. Besides, when people covered up doors they didn't leave the handle on, did they? She traces the dull brass handle with her fingers, surprised to find that it's icy cold.

She takes a step back, her legs unsteady, unsure what she wants to do next.

CHAPTER 10

Rachel leans close to the door, listening for any sound of the other side. All she hears is her own breathing, which is faster than it ought to be and ragged from the fear clenching her chest. She edges closer, reaching out with her hand to touch the wall.

The second she touches it, something knocks on the door from the other side. Hard and insistent. She jumps back, holding up the hammer defensively. The sound comes again, only this time she's ready for it. She lets out a short laugh, lowering the hammer. The knocking isn't coming from the door she uncovered, but from the cabin's front door.

"Hello?" calls John. "You in there? Everything all right?"

His voice carries through the cabin's walls as if they aren't even there. She can tell he's on the move from the front door to the back of the cabin. If he gets to the back he'll have a clear view of her little demolition project and she doesn't want that.

"Just a second," she says. She runs to the spare bedroom and rips a sheet off the bed. Back in the living room, she hangs the sheet on the ragged corners of her little demolition project so that the hole is covered up. There's still debris all over the floor, but at least it's something.

She hurries over to the front door and swings it open.

"Right here," she says, stepping out on the landing. John's already halfway down the length of the cabin, almost to the first windows, but he stops and walks back. "Sorry," she says, pretending to comb her hair back into place with her fingers. "I was taking a nap."

John grins. "Is that part of the writing process?"

"An essential one. Where do you think all the ideas come from?" Her voice comes out high and fast. She takes a steadying breath, trying to forget the door in the wall waiting for her inside. She notices he's carrying two grocery bags, one under each arm. "Making another delivery?" she says, trying to sound casual.

He holds the bags up. "Thought you could use some supplies."

She cranes her neck and steals a quick look inside. Milk, bread, lunchmeat, strawberries, a few other items on the bottom that she can't see. "Thank you. This is nice, but you don't need to keep bringing me food. I'm fine. Really."

John looks at her oddly. "You sure? Is everything all right in there?" he asks. "You have… I don't know… what is that?"

She looks down at her shirt and sees that it's covered with drywall dust. She's sure it's in her hair and on her face too.

"Flour," she says. "I was trying to make some pancakes or something. Got it everywhere."

John leans over and tries to look past her into the cabin. She moves to block him.

"Some pancakes or something?"

"I'll clean it up," she says. "Don't worry."

"What happened to the window?" he says, putting his foot on the first step leading up to the landing. She stands on the top of the stairs, blocking him.

"No big deal, really. And you know what, I'm right in the middle of writing an important scene. Do you think maybe you could do the whole landlord thing some other time?" She says it with a smile, but she knows she sounds guilty as hell.

"I thought you said you were making pancakes… or something," John says. "No, wait. You said you were taking a nap."

She closes the door behind her. "Here's the deal. I'm blocked. I'll admit that. I just need a little space, is all. You can understand that, right?"

John smiles and she notices just how damn good-looking he is.

"Sure, but what I don't get is how holing yourself up in there will help you. Seems to me the way to unblock yourself is to get out in the world. Take a break."

"That's what you think?"

"That is what I think." He takes another step up toward her, his tone deadly serious. "I have one word for you. Canoe."

"What's that?"

"Canoe. You know, two to three-person boat. Paddles. On the water." He makes broad motions like he's paddling a canoe. "There's one right by the dock."

She knows there is but all she can think about is the door waiting for her back inside the house. And what might be on the other side.

"Sorry, I really can't. Maybe a different day?" she suggests, hoping this will be enough to send him on his way.

He just shrugs and takes another step up the stairs, so close now that she takes a step back. "Okay, let me just do a quick check through the house and I'll be out of your hair."

"No," she says, a little too loudly. "I mean, sure. Let's take the canoe out. Maybe it'll help clear my head."

He grins. "What a great idea." He moves to squeeze past her on the stairs.

"Where are you going?"

"I was going to put these away first."

She grabs the bags and takes them from him. "I'll get these. Meet you down at the canoe."

John looks past her toward the door, then leans to the side to look through a window. "Now you have me nervous. You have something in there you don't want me to see?"

She laughs but it's loud and sounds nervous even to her own ears. "Just dirty underwear and bad writing," she says. "Trust me, I'm doing you a favor."

John holds up his hands in surrender. "You win. I'll meet you down there." He turns and strides down the side of the house, angling toward the canoe in the weeds down by the dock. He doesn't look left and so he never sees the new door she uncovered in the cabin's wall.

She follows him down, her anxiety about getting back to the door melting away into an unexpected emotion: relief. The door scares her. And the decision whether she ought to open it or not is not a forgone conclusion. This gives her time to think it over and, hopefully, make the right decision on what to do.

Getting the canoe down to the water takes the two of them. They spend a couple of minutes picking out weeds, dead leaves and a few bugs from inside the boat. John produces two life jackets but they're both eaten away by mold and smell like compost, so they opt out.

"Promise not to capsize us?" John asks.

"I make no promises. I haven't been out on a canoe since I was a little girl."

They push the canoe's nose into the water and she jumps in while she's still on dry land, crawling forward as she keeps her weight center-balanced.

"Just remember small moves," John says as he pushes them the rest of the way into the water and jumps in the back. "Small moves and smooth strokes."

"Uh... with what?"

They look back to the shore where the two paddles are still on the shore. John hangs his head, but he's smiling. "Never said I was good at this. Stay right here."

He rolls over the side of the canoe and into the water. It's shallow, only up to his knees and he's wearing shorts. He trudges through the water back to shore, grabs the paddles and makes his way back.

"What kept you?" she says.

"Now she gets a sense of humor," he says, rocking the canoe as if to tip it over. He hands her one of the paddles and climbs back in. "Okay, like I was saying, small moves, easy strokes."

She dips her paddle in the water. The lake is weirdly clear and she can see the rocky bottom slip by as they get under way. Neither of them says anything as they find their stroke, matching each other's timing, and the canoe slices through the water. The sun comes out from behind a cloud and she pauses long enough to turn her face toward it with her eyes closed, soaking in the warmth.

"Nice, right?" John says.

It's not really a question, more of a statement, but she answers anyway. "Nice," she says, turning back to look at him. The strange door in the cabin and the pile of shredded drywall seem distant, like something imagined.

"I like to see you smile," he says. "Not sure if I've seen that since you've been here."

She turns back around and resumes her paddling. "Maybe you're just not very funny, ever think of that?"

He laughs. "You know, that never crossed my mind. But now that you mention it, it explains a lot in my life."

She laughs at the comment and they paddle without speaking, surprised that the silence is so comfortable. The exercise feels good too. Her shoulders start to burn from the repetitive motion but she doesn't want to be the first to stop. They're almost to the far end of the lake before he says something and it gives her an excuse to take a rest.

"So, what are you writing about?" he asks.

It's an innocuous question, but in her blocked state it sounds like an accusation. She takes a breath and centers herself.

"I'd rather not talk about it," she says.

"Would you rather talk about how the window in the cabin got broken?"

"Third option?" she asks.

"We can always talk about the weather. That's usually safe."

"The weather, huh? Okay, you start."

"So, what kinds of things do you write about when it's sunny with a slight breeze out of the west?"

She hits the water with her paddle and splashes him.

"Nice try. How about you? What do you do when you're not showing up unannounced at your rental property with emergency rations for your guests?"

"Oh, I have several properties. I just move back and forth offering canoe tours. This is my third ride of the day."

"The whole not-being-funny-thing, that really doesn't stop you from trying, does it?"

He laughs and it feels warm like the sun.

"Just a numbers game. Enough jokes per minute and something's bound to hit home."

"So that's your thing? Being quirky."

"My thing?"

"You know, the thing you use to get through it all. Some people are smart-asses. Some are paranoid."

"And you think I'm quirky?"

"Without a doubt," she says. "Writers have keen powers of observation so our conclusions carry more weight than those of you mere mortals."

"I see how it is," John says. "I can live with quirky. Better than dorky, I guess."

"Oh, it's a fine line."

John laughs again and it feels so familiar that it pulls at something in her chest. She tries to place it, maybe an old friend with a similar laugh, but she can't grab on to the thread. And then it's gone.

"So what's your thing?"

"How's that?" she says.

"Your thing. Your navigation tool through the world."

Her smile fades. A dark cloud drifts across the sun, casting a cold shadow over them.

"I don't think I know anymore," she says, surprised at her honesty with this stranger.

"That's the risk, isn't it?" John says. If her serious tone had thrown him off, he doesn't show it.

"How do you mean?"

"You said it yourself, writers have these keen powers of observation. Observe too much and it's easy to forget you've been put on this earth to be a participant."

"Yeah, well there are worse things than forgetting."

"I don't know about that. Everything we do, everything that happens to us makes us who we are," he says. "Forgetting something, even something bad, reduces us. Erodes who we are at the edges. Forget enough and that erosion can go to your core."

She turns to look at him, wobbling the canoe as she does. "Someone's been reading too many fortune cookies."

He shrugs. "It's what I believe."

She nods, realizing he's being serious. Before she can stop herself, she hears herself say exactly what she's thinking, without filter. "And what if you don't like who you are? What if your experiences create a person you don't like? What then?"

John looks away and she could swear his eyes are welled with tears. He takes several moments, collecting himself, and she finds herself wishing she could take the words back.

"What are we going to do with you?" he says.

"That's not an answer."

John stands up in the canoe, the boat rocking as he balances.

"What are you doing?" she asks, grabbing the side rails of the canoe.

"Giving you an answer."

He jumps off the canoe, nearly capsizing it. It's an ungainly leap, arms and legs flailing. He disappears under the water and then comes up whooping like a kid who just conquered a mountain.

"Wow! That's cold as shit!" he yells.

"What are you doing?" she says, bewildered but laughing.

He swims to the side of the canoe and holds on to the edge. The water must be cold because he's out of breath, but God he looks alive. "You wanted your answer. Come on in."

"No thanks, I'm fine right here," she says. "You're the quirky one, remember?"

John shrugs. "Suit yourself. I'll just climb back in."

"Wait... you're going to..."

The canoe tips from his weight and she falls into the water. The shock of the cold wakes up every sense in her body. There's someone screaming under the water. It's not even muffled, but shrill and heartrending. But then it's gone, replaced by the sound of quiet sobbing, so personal and deep that she feels embarrassed to hear it. Then that too is gone. And there's silence. Wrapping around her like a blanket. So pure that she wants to stay there and just be part of it.

Then a strong hand grabs her arm and pulls her upward. When she breaks the surface, she blinks back the water and squints at the sun. John has one hand on the canoe and the other holding her.

"Are you all right? I'm so sorry, I didn't mean to do that," he says.

She gently pulls away from him and treads water. "I'm fine." She takes stock of herself, surprised to find she's telling the truth. Whatever had happened seconds earlier under water has passed through her and left her untouched. She feels a warm contentment spread through her. Like the cathartic afterglow of a good cry. "I feel good, actually."

"You scared me to death. I thought you'd forgotten how to swim."

She turns on her back and executes a perfect backstroke. "Serves you right," she says.

Her clothes cling to her skin and she's getting colder so she knows she can't stay in long. But she can't tell what she's enjoying more, the impromptu swim or watching him squirm. She decides to let him off the hook and gives him a wide smile. "Dangerously close to being dorky instead of quirky though. Just saying."

John laughs. He manages to turn the capsized canoe right side up and swims toward the shore, towing it with the bowline rope in his hand. He appears not to be in any hurry and she notices him watching her swim. She looks up and there's not a cloud in the sky.

CHAPTER 11

A couple of hours later, the sun has set and they're back at the cabin, sitting opposite one another around a campfire. Rachel's changed out of her wet clothes and she's wrapped in a bulky sweater, relishing the warmth. The cup of whiskey with a splash of coffee in it doesn't hurt either.

John's across from her, hazy in the rising heat from the fire, accented by periodic bursts of sparks. She stares into the flames, lost in their dance.

"Is the fire all right with you?" he asks.

She nods. "Feels good."

A long pause, perfectly empty except for the gentle sounds of the fire.

"When's the last time you did it?" John asks.

She nearly spits her drink into the fire. "What?"

John laughs. "Enjoying your time with your mind in the gutter over there?"

"That's where my mind is most comfortable," she says, masking her embarrassment.

"I was talking about writing."

She takes a drink. "Well, either way, it's been a while."

"Since you've done it, or done it well?"

There's a pause and then they both burst out laughing.

"Writing," he says. "C'mon now."

"You said it," she says. God, it feels good to laugh. To feel normal. He seems to give up the line of questioning and they sit quietly, as patient as the stars inching across the sky.

"How about you?" she finally asks, realizing it's more than small talk. She really wants to know the answer. "How'd you end up out here?"

"Nothing complicated. Fell for a girl. A really great girl."

"Ah, the downfall of all men."

John's voice is distant, like he didn't hear her. "She always wanted a place like this. Even before we found this spot, she could describe it to me perfectly. Like she'd been here before and just couldn't remember how to get back."

"So where's this girl?"

John stares into the fire and shakes his head. There are no details in the action, only the unmistakable look of heartbreak.

"I'm sorry," she says.

He nods. "Part of her is still here, you know. As long as that's true, I'll be here too."

A chorus of howls rises up in the distance. Her head jerks up at the sound.

"Maybe we should head inside," she says, her mouth suddenly dry. She has no interest in facing another wolf, especially outside where she's exposed.

"They shouldn't bother us," John says. "Not this close to the house."

"I wouldn't count on that." She stands up and John follows her lead back to the deck and the sliding door. As they approach the door, she realizes she has to get rid of him. If he comes inside, her demolition project will be discovered. It's been a terrible mistake allowing herself to get too comfortable with him and now she's going to pay the price unless she can send him on his way. She turns and blocks him from coming in. "Thanks for a great afternoon. I really needed that."

John looks past her. The cabin inside is completely dark. "Do you have a lantern close by? Do you want me to..." He turns on a flashlight and shines it inside. He has it trained on the sheet covering the wall she destroyed earlier that day. "What's that?"

Her stomach sinks at the idea of him seeing the hole, but there's no stopping him now. As he gently but firmly edges past her and enters the cabin, she's already in full excuse-making mode.

"I can explain," she says.

He's at the sheet, looking behind it with the flashlight.

"I'll pay for the repairs," she says.

He yanks on the sheet and it falls to the ground. The wall is intact. The hole gone. The floor clean of debris.

Like nothing ever happened.

"Pay to repair what?" John asks.

Rachel's arms cross her stomach on reflex. The shock of seeing the wall leaves her nauseous and unsteady on her feet. It's impossible. She steps up to the wall and touches it. She expects it to be soft like the repaired bullet holes. Or have some indication that someone had been there to patch the hole while John distracted her. But there's no evidence of that. The drywall looks aged. Stained from old water leaks. Chipped and worn.

"Are you all right?" John asks.

"No," she replies. "I don't think I am. It's just... just... I need to be alone."

"If you tell me what it is, maybe I can help you," John says, taking her hand in his. "Tell me what you see."

She shakes her head and pulls her hand back. "Please. Just leave me alone. I need some time to think."

"What if I—"

"Please."

"Just let me—"

THE TORMENT OF RACHEL AMES

"What the fuck is wrong with you?" she yells. "I need to be alone. What's so goddamn hard to understand about that?"

John holds his hands up and backs away. "Okay. You're right. My fault." His voice is soothing and it makes her feel like she's a wild animal he's trying to calm down. "I'm leaving. I'm sorry."

She takes a shuddering breath. "I'm sorry. It's just that—"

"You don't need to explain anything," he says. "It's fine." He goes to the sliding door and then pauses. "Can I check on you tomorrow?"

She smiles and nods. "That would be nice."

He hesitates like he has more to say, but thinks better of it. He leaves and closes the sliding door behind him.

She walks across to the other side of the cabin and peers out the window in the kitchen that gives her a view of where her own car is parked. Next to it, she sees a white pickup truck. John comes into view from her left, flashlight bobbing along as he walks. But when he gets to the pickup, he goes to the passenger side and opens the door. The dome light comes on and the driver jerks up like he's been asleep.

It's Ollie.

What the hell was he doing there?

She turns, feeling her grasp on reality turning to sand between her fingers. The claw hammer is on the kitchen counter next to her. She grabs it and, holding the lantern in the other hand, goes into the living room. She stands in front of the

94

wall, the swaying lantern sending her shadow around the room.

"I'm not going crazy," she says.

She looks at her reflection staring back at her in the sliding glass door.

"Right?"

Her reflection has nothing to say. So she turns to the wall and, with a yell, digs the claw into the drywall.

The excavation goes quicker this time, and once she uncovers a section of the door beneath, she's certain she's done this before. The drywall comes off in large chunks as she powers through it. It's not long before she can step back and stand in front of the exposed door once again.

Only now there's no handle.

And she's sure there was one before.

She brushes off the area where the door handle should be and finds two holes filled with soft plaster. She feels all around the perimeter of the door, digging in her fingers, trying to grip the edge to pull it open. When that doesn't work, she drops to her knees, ignoring the pain of the chunks of drywall digging into her skin. She holds the lantern close and inspects the gap under the door. It's too narrow to see anything on the other side, but as she watches a draft comes from under the door and pushes the dust from the drywall forward. There's a pause and then the draft reverses direction, sucking air under the door. Then back out. In. Out.

Like it's breathing.

She levers the claw end of the hammer under the door and yanks on it. The door doesn't budge. She hits the door with the hammer. Standing up, she kicks it, punches it with her fist. Losing control.

"Open up, you son-of-a-bitch," she screams. "Open the door. Let me out of here."

She drops the hammer to the floor and staggers backward.

"To hell with this," she says under her breath.

Kicking drywall debris out of her way, she goes to the kitchen and opens the cupboard door. There, lined up four across and three deep, are bottles of Jack Daniels. Way more than she brought with her. Whoever is messing with her, fixing walls, cleaning up debris, must have planted these too. At least they had the decency to have her brand. She pulls a bottle out, twists off the top and guzzles it down. It pours out faster than she can handle so it drips from her mouth and down her front. She turns as she drinks, wondering if the wall will be back in place again and she'll really have lost her mind.

She drops the bottle and it shatters on the floor.

The door is wide open.

CHAPTER 12

Rachel walks slowly to the door, glancing
nervously around the room in case something
had opened it from the other side and crept out
into the room, hiding in the shadows, waiting to
pounce. But the room looks undisturbed.
Underwood is still there and she puts a reassuring
hand on him as she walks past. Despite their
recent failure to see eye-to-eye, he's still her oldest
friend and the cool touch of his steel frame
steadies her.

She puts the lantern on the table to make
the shadows in the room stand still. She's already
creeped out enough without the extra
atmospherics. There's a stone landing on the other

side of the door that extends about ten feet before plunging down into a curved staircase. A red glow comes up from below, pulsing in the unmistakable cadence of a heartbeat. A hot wind blows out from the passageway, sending her hair billowing out behind her. It smells of charred and burnt things.

She considers trying to find her gun, but something tells her that a weapon like that would be pointless. The smart thing to do is close the door, repair the wall and forget this whole thing ever happened. Probably best to get in her car and get the hell out of Dodge while she was at it. But she couldn't, not when she was so close. She had to know what was in there.

"On a whim, out on a limb," she says out loud to the empty room, wondering just how far out on the limb she'll go before it breaks off and she falls forever downward.

Leaving the lantern behind, she walks through the door, feeling the heat grow more intense when she crosses the threshold.

The second she's through, the door slams shut behind her.

She's gone...

...and the cabin's silent. The lantern burns, casting its stark light. Slowly the flame in the lantern shrinks, like someone is turning a dial toward the off position. The shadows deepen and darkness fills the corners of the room.

A muffled scream comes from far away, somehow below the floor. Then the cabin vibrates like it's sitting on top of an enormous engine that just started up. Dust shakes loose from the ceiling. Underwood shudders, its keys clacking in place. There's a jolt and the cabin lurches to the side like in an earthquake.

The sudden sound of footsteps and screaming...

...and the door bursts open. Rachel tumbles to the floor, clothes shredded, face bloodied. She turns and pushes back from the now open door.

Up the stairs comes the black wolf, the same one that attacked her before. Its hackles are up. Teeth bared. Strands of drool drip from its mouth.

It snarls, claws grating against the stone floor. It crouches down, ready to spring.

She yells and flies at the door, slamming it shut just as the wolf lunges.

The wolf smashes against the door. Snarling, barking. Claws digging into the wood. But the door holds.

She turns and braces against the attack with all her strength. She'll do anything to keep the door shut. Anything to lock the monster inside.

She sags to the ground, her back pressed as hard as she can against the door. Sobbing. The same words tumbling from her lips over and over.

I'm sorry.
I'm sorry.
I'm sorry.

Chapter 13

Day.
Rachel turns to the window, surprised to see the sun's already past its zenith and settling low in the sky. Surprised because she can't remember it coming up. She's still on the floor, still braced against the door even though it's been hours since she's heard the wolf. Her eyes are red from crying and lack of sleep. She feels like a shell, a thin husk of herself capable of being destroyed by nothing more than a breeze.

Moving carefully, every muscle and joint screaming in pain, she stands up while keeping her body pressed against the wall. Slowly, she turns and can't help but laugh at what she sees.

The wall has been repaired.

And there's no sign of the door.

She laughs harder and she worries that she might never be able to stop unless she gets out of the cabin. Unless she gets as far from this place as possible.

But even as she has the thought, she knows she's not going anywhere. Something has clicked inside of her, a part of her that needs to understand what's going on. Somehow she senses it's important that she uncovers the truth, that it's essential. And she knows exactly where she needs to go to get answers.

She tries to run outside but has to settle for a jog instead because her sore body slows her down. She doesn't even want to imagine what her bruised skin must look like under her clothes.

She manhandles the canoe back to the water, climbs in and paddles hard toward Granger's cabin. She makes the trip across the lake in good time, fired up by her rising anger. Granger knows what's going on, might even be responsible for it somehow. By the time the canoe beaches on the far shore, her arms and back are tired but her anger hasn't slacked at all.

Granger's place looks like a log cabin from a distance, but up close it's an amalgamation of found objects. Logs, bark, rocks, rusted sheets of corrugated metal, the seams packed with mud and moss. The roof sags and looks about to fall in. Chickens hunt and peck around the burn piles of trash that litter the property. Ropes strung between trees hold the drying pelts of raccoon, rabbit, squirrel and fox. A thin tendril of smoke rises from an old campfire.

"Granger!" she calls out. "Are you here?"

She passes the campfire with its two chairs and scattering of chicken bones and goes to the cabin's front door.

"Hello?" she calls as she knocks on the door.

The door edges open when she touches it. "Granger? Are you in here?" She pushes it open all the way.

It's dark inside and, knowing how odd the old bastard is, she's not excited by the idea of going in uninvited. But her anger gives way to her good nature as she pictures Granger on the floor of the cabin clutching his chest from a heart attack. Or even lying there with a broken hip. She has a flash image of Professor McNeely sprawled on her college classroom floor, feet kicking, stain spreading out from his crotch, his body fighting all the way to the end.

"Hello?" she calls out again as she steps inside. The single room cabin is in shambles, the den of a pack rat. Old machine parts, tools, animal traps, stacks of animal pelts. Hundreds of animal antlers cover the walls, many with the skull of the animal attached, vacant eye sockets staring into the room. Suspended from string, a flock of stuffed birds hangs from the ceiling. Crows, ravens, finches, all covered with dust, some with feathers eaten away by mold. Death everywhere but no sign of the old man.

"Granger," she says, about ready to give up the search.

Then something grabs her from behind. She screams and turns around, knowing it's the black wolf, ready to strike her down.

But it's not the wolf, it's Granger. "Got you again. Never seen someone jump so high." He's bent over, laughing.

"Damn it," she says. "What the hell's wrong with you?"

"Jus' havin' a little fun, is all," Granger says, laying the New England accent on heavy. "'Sides, you're the one pokin' 'round up in 'ere."

"I thought you might be in trouble, asshole," she says.

"What? Dead of a heart attack or something?" Granger says. "Wouldn't that be something?"

She takes a deep breath to calm herself but the musty air makes her cough.

"What? Don't like the place? Lacks a woman's touch is what I think," Granger says. "Let's go outside. Sure you didn't come over here unless there was somethin' on your mind."

He gestures towards the door and she walks outside, more than ready to get away from the cabin and all the dead animals. Granger follows her out to the chairs by the smoldering campfire and adds a couple of logs. A few minutes later, the wood blazes as they face each other in the two chairs.

"So, anything exciting happen at work today, dear?" Granger says.

"I want some answers."

"What? No foreplay?"

"The first time we met—"

"You mean the first time I scared the shit out of you."

"Right. You said something that night that's stayed with me. About the cabin."

"The cabin. So, it's happening already, is it?"

"What? What's happening?"

Granger gets up from his chair, picks up a long stick and uses it to poke the fire, sending a shower of sparks up into the darkening sky. "Hard to know," he says. "It's different every time. Why don't you tell me what's happening?"

"There's a door."

"Go on." Granger reaches down to the ground and scoops up a rooster walking past him. The rooster fusses a little, but then rests comfortably tucked under Granger's arm as he strokes the bird's head.

"I found this door, a hidden door. Somehow, I knew the door was there even though it was hidden, if that makes any sense. Like it was calling to me."

"Did you open the door?"

"Once." She recalls the wall being intact when she left the cabin. "I think."

Granger sits back down heavily in his chair, the rooster in his lap like an accessory dog used by a Hollywood starlet. "Lady, either you opened it or you didn't. Which is it?"

"I don't know. I keep having these dreams. They're so real that I think I'm someplace else, but then things... change back... like they were before."

"Someplace else? Where do you go?"

"You don't know what's going on either, do you?" she says, her voice cracking. She stands up. "This is ridiculous."

"Sit down!" Granger barks. The words come out as a command and she sits out of instinct. Granger stares at her while he pets the rooster on his lap, which seems more than happy to just sit there. Granger's eyes screw up like he's in a windstorm only he can feel.

She shifts uncomfortably. "Why are you looking at me like that?"

"I'm just trying to figure you out."

"Great, that makes two of us. This all has to make sense somehow."

"Make sense? Why? Are you one of those people who believes everything has a purpose?"

"I don't have time for this," she snaps. She considers that she might have been wrong to come to this place. Maybe Granger didn't know anything after all.

"You said you want to know what's going on," Granger says, his voice laced with anger. "I'm trying to tell you."

She leans back in her chair, breathes deep and nods for Granger to continue.

"Now, I'll ask you again, do you believe everything has a purpose?"

"I don't know. I used to, but..."

"Now you're not so sure."

"Something like that."

Granger grins wickedly. "Welcome to the club, my girl. The Society of Miserable Sons-A-Bitches." He places the rooster on his head. "You get a funny hat and everything."

She smiles in spite of herself.

Granger kisses the rooster, puts it back on his lap and strokes it gently. "There, that's better. Maybe now you're ready to listen. Because what I'm about to tell you is the most important thing you're ever going to hear."

"Somehow I doubt that," she says.

Granger ignores the comment. "There are immutable rules to the universe that cannot be circumvented. That cannot be suspended no matter how clever you are, how beautiful you are, how wretched you are."

She shifts uncomfortably in her chair. Granger watches her closely.

"So, you know what I'm talking about."

She laughs but it comes out hollow and false. "Not a clue."

Granger looks smug. "That's not true. You see clues of the truth every day. Sure, maybe you can't describe it in words, but you can feel it, can't you? Sure you can. Every human can on some level. Right at the edge of consciousness. Something so pure and unalterable, that it's

106

terrifying. So absolute that you can't bring yourself to acknowledge it no matter how much you want to. Tell me you can't feel it."

"All I feel is that I'm losing my mind."

"Losing your mind? Shit, that would be a blessing, wouldn't it? The mind is our worst enemy." He nods to his lap where the rooster sits, allowing itself to be pet. "Imagine. To be like this bird here. No worries. No shame. No guilt." Granger tickles the rooster's neck with his thick, dirty fingers. "He's not thinking about tomorrow. He's just thinking that it feels good where he's at so he'll stay there. Pretty soon he'll have urges. Maybe to eat. Drink. Shit. Maybe he'll fuck one of them plump chickens over there."

Granger bends down and kisses the rooster on the head. Then he grabs it by the neck and twists. The rooster spasms violently, then goes limp. Granger opens his hands. "And just like that, maybe he won't."

"What the hell?" she cries out, shocked by the sudden violence. Bile rises in the back of her throat as she stares at the dead bird's broken neck. "Why'd you do that?"

Granger stands. "Because this animal lives by the rules. Life comes and then it is gone. Nothing to be down about that. Same rules apply to all of us."

Granger tosses the bird on her lap. She bats it away and it lands on the ground. "Besides, I'm hungry and that's dinner." He walks toward the house. "Make sure you get all them feathers off. Nothing spoils dinner like feathers in your teeth."

Chapter 14

Rachel watches Granger disappear inside the cabin. She nudges the dead chicken with her foot, fighting down her revulsion at the man's violence toward the poor animal. She looks over her shoulder at the canoe waiting on the shore behind her and considers making a break for it. Paddling straight across the lake and then a short walk to her car followed by a fast ride the hell out of there. But something stops her. Granger knows more than he's told her, she knows he does. The same way she knew there was a door hidden in the cabin walls. She decides that if putting up with Granger's special brand of crazy is what it takes to find out what's really going on, then so be it.

She bends down and picks up the dead chicken. With one long look at the cabin, she takes a handful of feathers and pulls.

An hour later, the sun now set, the chicken turns on a spit, roasting over the campfire. Granger kneels and shakes salt onto the meat.

"What do you know about the cabin?" she asks.

Granger peels off a piece of meat and takes a bite, then rotates the spit. He eyes Rachel, sizing her up. "Not quite ready yet. A little while longer, I think." He sits back in his chair, watching the fire.

"I've been thinking about your little speech," she says. "About the rooster."

"And?"

"And it's bullshit."

Granger's eyes narrow. "Really? Enlighten me."

"Our minds, our capacity to think, to feel, to remember, that's all that makes us human. Without that, we're reduced to animals."

"Reduced? It's a biological truth that we are animals, like it or not."

"We're more than animals," she says. "Or we at least have the capacity to be. Trying to block out the past is like blocking the sun with your hand. You can convince yourself you made the sun disappear, but you didn't. It burns whether you look right at it or not. How's that for a rule?"

"The sun, huh? That's pretty. You should be a writer."

She stands. "I want to understand what's going on here. These wolves, bizarre birds, Ollie sweeping leaves in the woods."

Granger doesn't look happy at the mention of Ollie's name but he lets it slide. He shakes his head sadly, like he's taking pity on her. "I used to be just like you. I did. But I fixed it." Granger leans forward. "What if I told you I could show you how to get rid of the past once and for all? Not just block the sun, but destroy it?"

Granger reaches behind his chair and pulls out a small brown bottle without a label.

"What are you talking about?"

"What if I had the power to take all your pain, all your memory of pain, all of it, and make it disappear forever?"

"There's no way you can do that," she whispers.

"I asked you what if I could? Would you take the deal? Would you make that bargain with me?"

Wolves howl in the distance. A wind stirs the trees. The fire blazes higher, spitting sparks into the night sky.

"The nightmares would be gone."

She hears sirens in the distance. People shouting. The smell of a fire. She puts her hands to the sides of her head to try to block it out.

"I can make it all go away."

"All of it?"

"All of it."

Three wolves appear on the edge of the forest, hackles up, eyes glowing with the fire's reflection. She sees the wolves and looks back at Granger.

"If you could promise me that..."

There's movement at the edge of her vision and she turns back toward the wolves. From behind them walks a small, blond boy in shorts and a Star Wars t-shirt. His skin is tanned and, even in the dark she can see his piercing blue eyes. The boy stops between the wolves and stares at her.

"The pain," Granger says. "Think of the pain."

She stands and stumbles toward the boy. "Little boy. What are you doing? You can't be here. Come to me. Nice and slow."

The boy turns and runs into the forest.

Granger grabs her by the shoulder and spins her around. "No more nightmares. No more pain. You can forget forever."

"Didn't you see that boy?" she says, pulling away. "He can't be here."

She runs toward the forest, finds the trail where the boy disappeared and sprints down it. The trees close in around her and block out the moon. Enough light filters through the branches that she can see the boy far ahead of her. She catches only the smallest glimpse of him before he disappears around a bend in the path.

"Stop! It's not safe out here," she yells.

The path narrows, walls of briar and stinging nettles pushing in from either side, encasing the trees that rise up to form a canopy overhead. Decaying logs lie across the path, some big enough that she has to crawl over them on her stomach. She's not sure how the boy could be outpacing her, but he is. On top of one fallen log she has a good view ahead and she spots him ducking down a side trail, the ferns so thick that they close in behind him as he passes.

"Wait!"

She runs harder, falls and scrapes her knees. Back up on her feet, she sprints after him, the branches ripping her clothes and scratching her skin as she passes. The trail suddenly opens up onto a meadow ringed with ancient trees. A low-lying fog covers the ground, glowing in the moonlight; thick and swirling like a living thing. She runs through it, drawing a vortex of fog behind her. She can't see the ground with the fog coming up to her chest.

"Where are you?" she shouts.

She looks behind her and sees three wolves in the tree line, their eyes glowing red. They leap into the meadow, disappearing as they run into the fog. All she can see are ripples just under the mist's surface as they run toward her.

She hurtles forward, stumbling blindly over the uneven ground. She gets to the end of the meadow and bolts down a path. She takes one turn and slides to a stop in front of a wall of fallen trees.

On every branch is an enormous black crow. Hundreds of them. They turn in unison to look at her and she sees they're not crows at all. They're all like the bird she killed at the cabin, a head of red skin with human lips and wide staring eyes. Only these don't have their mouths sewn shut. These have their lips curled back to reveal sharp, bloodstained teeth.

A cluster of them are on the ground in front of the tree, piled up as they scramble and fight over something. They turn to look at her and she sees they are feasting on the bloody carcass of the fawn she saw her first day at the cabin.

She screams and runs the other direction. The second she does, the birds explode into high-pitched shrieks that fill the forest.

She runs, desperate to find the boy. Just as desperate to get away from the birds.

There's a snarl from the path ahead of her. The black wolf steps forward, blocking her way.

She runs to her right, creating her own path through the dense growth. The brambles scrape across her skin. Vines wrap around her legs and she has a pulse of terror that the forest itself has come alive.

But the ground gives way downhill and she breaks free. She loses her balance and tumbles down it, protecting her head with her arms. All she can hear are the screams from the birds. The snarls of the wolves closing in. The sirens from the fire trucks and first responders. The roar of the fire. She rolls to a stop but stays on the ground, her hands clutching her head, covering her ears, useless. They have her this time. There's no escape. No need to even try. She curls up in a ball and waits for the end to come.

"Rachel. Thank God," says a voice. "She's over here."

She feels an arm around her and the voice, John's voice, is right next to her ear.

"It's all right. I'm right here. I'm right here."

She leans into him and squeezes her eyes tight. Slowly, like someone turning down the volume on a radio, the noises in her head fade. Soon, it's just white noise, a steady, unrelenting sound in the background.

"Come on," John says. "Let's get you out of here."

She gets to her feet, holding on to John's arm. She's surprised to see a second flashlight beam dancing nearby. It's Ollie and he looks scared.

"You okay, miss?" he asks as she passes him. "You aren't supposed to be out here on your own like this. Not how things work around here."

She stops. Her body shakes from the adrenaline surge from the chase, but she ignores it. She stares at Ollie. "You said that before. What's that supposed to mean?"

Ollie looks confused and more frightened all at the same time. He looks to John for help.

"Come on," John says. "You've been through a lot. Let's get back to the cabin. We can talk there."

115

"No, I want to know what he means," she says, her voice trembling. "Just how are things supposed to work around here?"

Ollie turns off his flashlight as if that will make him invisible. "Sorry, miss," he says from the dark. "That's not for me to say."

John pulls her toward him until he's whispering in her ear. "Let's just get back to the cabin. And I'll tell you what you want to know. I promise."

Chapter 15

Rachel sits on the weathered old couch in the living room, watching John closely as he pours them all coffee. Every one of his movements stirs a gnawing sense of premonition in her chest. She gives the wall the barest of glances. As she expects, there's no sign of a door or any damage to the drywall.

"You gave us a scare, is all," Ollie says. "How did you even get out there?"

John walks behind him and puts a hand on his shoulder as if to quiet him. Ollie looks apologetic and waves away the offered mug of coffee. John hands a cup to her and sits next to her on the couch. The way he looks at her twists a knot in her stomach and she can't figure out why.

"We should go," Ollie says. "Let her get some rest."

"Stay," she says. "You said we would talk. You promised me something."

John hesitates, then nods. "I'll catch up with you later, Ollie."

Ollie doesn't mask that he doesn't like what's happening, but whatever complaint he has about it, he swallows and heads for the door. She follows and watches out of the window as he climbs into his pickup truck and drives away. She turns back to John and looks at him with her head cocked to one side.

"Why are you looking at me like that?" he asks from across the cabin.

"It just occurred to me that you didn't even ask me what I saw out there."

"Do you want to tell me about it?"

She looks back out the window, raw doubt eating at her stomach. "How long did you say you've owned this place?"

"What's that?" He seems surprised by the change of direction.

"How long have you owned this cabin?"

"I don't know. Years."

"How many years?"

"Oh, I don't know. Why?"

"Would you say five years? Ten?"

"Something like that." He puts down his coffee. "Look, whatever you got into out there tonight shook you up pretty good. How about you head to bed? I'll sleep out here to make sure everything's all right and we can talk tomorrow."

She walks to the kitchen and pulls open a drawer and wraps her hand around her gun. "So which do you think it is? Five or ten?" She pulls out the gun. "Seems odd that you wouldn't know."

"Does it really matter? I think—"

"I think it does matter," she says, walking toward him, raising the gun in front of her. "I think it really fucking matters."

John stands up, his hands out to either side. "Okay, let's just relax here."

"What have you been putting in my food?"

"What?"

"You brought food. Those drinks. There must be something in them. Right after I got here, it's when I started seeing things. And I can't... I can't remember things."

"Just put the gun down, all right? We're just talking here."

She cocks the gun. "How did I find this place?"

John swallows hard. "I had ads out all over the place. Internet mostly. You'd know better than I would."

"You're right. I should know," she says. "But I don't. Did I call you on the phone? Did we exchange emails about me renting this place?"

"You emailed me," he says, but he sounds like a kid lying. He's not good at it.

"Then why don't I remember that?"

"Put the gun down. Please. It's me."

"Why don't I remember?" The sound of sirens rises up from the soundtrack in her head.

"It's all right. Just calm down. You've been through a lot."

"Have I?" she says, her voice cracking. "I remember driving here but that's it. I don't remember finding this place. Or emailing you. It doesn't make any sense." She steps closer, gun shaking in her trembling hands. The sounds of emergency sirens louder now. "What are you doing to me? What's going on in this place?"

John's reaction isn't what she expects. Tears well in his eyes and his lower lip trembles. He slowly walks toward her, arms still open.

"Stop," she says, holding up the gun. "Stop right there."

But he doesn't stop. He gets closer and closer until the barrel of the gun is pressed up against his chest. Now tears track down his cheeks and he makes no move to wipe them away.

"I'm so sorry," he whispers.

"Who are you?" she asks again, barely able to get the words out. It feels like she's under water, unable to breathe. "Tell me what's happening."

He moves his hands slowly to her gun and she lets him take it. Once she lets go of it, the sirens fade. She puts a hand on his chest and feels his heart pounding.

Something deep inside her stirs and she moves her body closer to his. He just stands there, his breath shallow. His body trembling against hers.

She leans forward to kiss him and stops with their lips nearly touching.

"We can't," he says.

Their eyes connect, search for something and find it. She kisses him. The second she does, the soundtrack in her head clicks off.

He's hesitant at first, but that doesn't last. They kiss harder, their mouths craving each other. Bodies pressed together.

She pulls away, takes his hand and grabs a blanket from the couch. She pulls him to the sliding door and walks him outside.

They stand in front of one another, the full moon and a canopy of brilliant stars overhead. They slowly undress each other. Taking their time with each piece of clothing. Caressing. Kissing. Finally, they're naked, standing only inches apart, their skin glowing in the moonlight.

They stand there, not touching, but so close she can feel his warmth on her skin. John's fingers dance over her body, still not touching, tracing the contours of her breasts, her stomach, the small of her back. Finally, they reach for one another. Fingers caress every inch of bare skin. John's lips brush along her neck. Her shoulder. Tender. Slow. They move together and kiss, the urgency building, moving now as if they are unable to get close enough.

She pushes him backward and he lies down on the blanket, his eyes never leaving hers.

She straddles him and arches her back as she guides him into her. They move slowly at first, careful and delicate. But the need overtakes their caution and she quickens her rhythm. They're both panting now, groaning. She pulls his hands to her hips and lets him guide her thrusts. She wants him deeper inside of her. She wants all of him. And he's willing to give it.

CHAPTER 16

Rachel wakes up and sees light streaming through the bedroom windows. She feels John's heat in the bed next to her and his hand draped over her shoulder. Carefully, she slides out of bed without disturbing him, pulls on jeans and a sweater and leaves the room.

Underwood greets her, gleaming and well oiled. Keys ready to do her bidding, promising that if pressed in just the right order for just the right period of time, art might be created. For the first time in a long while, there's no sense of anxiety when she looks at the blank pages stacked next to the typewriter. There's a different emotion, unexpected in its simplicity and its purity.

Hope.

She sits down at the table, giving Underwood a slight nod in greeting before she plucks a blank sheet of paper from the pile. She feeds it into Underwood's roller and turns the wheel with confidence, none of the usual uncertainty in her movements today, and lines the paper up. Her fingers come to rest on the keys. They feel cool to the touch but familiar, like a handshake with an old friend.

"Good morning, Underwood," she whispers. "I've missed you."

Her fingers dance and the keys whip the paper in a blur of motion. Seconds later, a sentence of her thoughts exists on the page, the abstract made solid and real. She doesn't stop to read it or to think about what those words mean, she just tells her fingers to dance some more. And they do.

The cabin fills with a furious *rat-tat-tat*, staccato bursts of words that fill one page, then another. And another. Her hands cramp, out of practice, but she ignores it. This is the glorious flood after the dam breaks and she intends to ride it for as long as she can. The only two outside thoughts she allows in are that she looks forward to John waking up to share the moment with her. And that, aside from the sounds of the typewriter, the birdsong filtering in from outside and the story spinning from her head to her fingers, her mind is gloriously silent.

No sirens. No white noise of the fire burning. It's just her. Whole again.

An entire glorious hour passes before she allows herself to take a break. She stacks the finished pages on the table next to Underwood, stands and stretches, rubbing the knuckles of her hands. She scribbles a note to John on the cover page, *Read if you want.* She nearly decides to crumple the invitation, but she shrugs and leaves it there. She wants John to read it. Not her best work ever, but it's who she is and she wants to share that with him.

She opens the sliding door and the sound of singing birds doubles in volume. There's a slight breeze, just cool enough to make it pleasant. Cotton ball clouds drift overhead, backed by a perfect blue sky. She walks past the blanket on the ground and smiles, thinking for a second that she might go back inside to wake John up and reward herself for her morning writing session with a morning session of a different kind. But she knows that can wait. He's not going anywhere. Not on this perfect day with her typed pages on her desk and the beautiful silence in her head. This was exactly how things were supposed to be here at the cabin, the perfect place she'd always imagined in her mind.

She walks to the end of the short dock and sits on the edge, her feet hanging to the green-tinged water, and watches the world slowly pass by her. The sound of a door closing catches her attention and she feels her heart beat a little faster, like a schoolgirl whose crush just walked near. But she realizes the sound came from in front of her, not behind. She squints at Granger's cabin across the way and sees the old man walking toward the water's edge, binoculars up to his face. She's feeling mischievous so she waves at him to make sure she has his attention, then flashes him the middle finger, first on one hand, then adding the other for a double air-pumping F-you. The old man lowers his binoculars, turns and goes back to his cabin.

"Yeah, you better run away," she says.

The sliding door opens behind her and John steps outside. She waves at him, wondering if he saw her flipping off the neighbor. She notices her typed pages in his hand and she immediately regrets her note telling him he could read it. First draft work isn't meant for human consumption, she knows that. What felt like pure poetry coming out could turn to complete shit within hours of being written. But as he walks up to her, the fear that it hadn't been any good melts away. John holds the pages tenderly, like they are a sacred thing, his eyes red and swollen as if he's been crying. He sits next to her on the dock, but says nothing. Finally, it's too much for her to bear.

"Did you like it?" she asks.

She feels his body trembling next to her.

"He was beautiful," he says, the words no more than a whisper. "The boy you wrote about."

She's confused by the reaction. She pulls back from him. "Are you all right?"

"Last night," he says. "That broke the rules. I'm not allowed to stay. But I'll be back. I promise."

"Rules? What are you talking about?" The words *but I'll be back* mean he's leaving. She can't stand that idea. Not when everything is perfect now. She stands up, angry. "Whose rules?"

John gets to his feet and takes her hands. "There's something I want to tell you," he says. "I think you're ready to hear the truth."

She shakes her head. A day ago she wanted the truth, now she just wants whatever last night was. Whatever this morning was. That was truth enough for her.

She steps away, leaving him alone at the end of the dock. He looks frightened and unsure with the pages she wrote that morning clutched in his hands.

"I have to tell you."

"No," she says, backing away. There's a distant sound of a siren, so real that it can't be just in her head. There's a siren and it's coming her way. It's coming because someone called for it in panic. It's rushing toward her in the hope that it's not too late. But it is too late. Because every time it comes, it's too late.

"Rachel, you know who I am." He holds up the pages in his hand. "It's right here."

"It's too late," she whispers. "It's too late every time."

"No, it's not," he replies softly. "We can do this. We can leave this place together. All you have to do is—"

She knows what's going to happen even before the bullet arrives. Some premonition causes

127

her to look over at Granger's cabin in time to see the flash when the old man fires his rifle. Time turns elastic and stretches out all around her. She hears the sound next and turns back to John. She wants to lunge forward and knock him out of the way, but she can't move. All she can do is watch with the horrible knowledge of what's about to happen.

The front of John's chest explodes in a spray of blood and bone, coating the dock in front of him. He lurches forward, but steadies himself, still standing. He looks at her with pleading eyes, reaches for her, then teeters backward and falls into the water.

She screams and runs to the end of the dock.

Bloody pages of her manuscript float on the water. No sign of John.

She dives in and swims for the bottom. Her eyes are open but she can't see anything. Frantic, she flails her arms, searching for him. Her lungs start to burn as her oxygen gives out.

She kicks to the surface, sucks in another breath and dives back down to the bottom.

It's not until her air runs out again that she feels the soft flesh of John's arm. She grabs it and pulls him toward the surface, choking, fighting her body's impulse to open her mouth to breathe.

They break the surface and she gasps for air. John slips through her fingers and starts to sink, but she grabs him. Grunting from the effort, she pulls him toward the shore, getting a foothold on the shallow bottom just when she thinks she can't go any farther. She drags him onto the small beach. His chest and stomach are drenched in blood, but his eyes open and they meet hers.

"I'm... sorry..." he mumbles.

She ignores him, takes his hands and puts them on the exit wound in his chest. "Press tight. Right here. I'm getting the car."

He says something to her but she's already running toward her Honda. The keys are in the ignition and she cranks the motor and throws it into drive. She mows over the bushes in her way and pulls the car alongside John's body. She climbs out and somehow finds the strength to pull him into the backseat of the car. By the time she's done, slick, hot blood covers her hands and her arms up to her elbows.

She climbs in, puts the Honda back into drive and peels out in the soft ground. John groans as she bumps roughly through the bushes and slides into the turn to take the short road back to the main road.

"Hang in there," she calls out to the backseat. She adjusts the rearview mirror so that it shows John. His face is white, covered with beads of sweat, eyes rolling around unfocused. "Press on it," she says. "Press on it hard."

They hit the highway and her foot jams the accelerator to the floor. The car reacts slowly but speed builds, topping out at ninety-five miles per hour. The trees on either side fly by in a blur. There are no other cars so she drives in the center of the road, devouring the white lines that whip past her so fast they look solid. Ahead the clouds churn in the sky, dark and menacing. She ignores them and drives.

"Hold on. I'm going to get you to a hospital."

She glances in the mirror. John's lost consciousness, his head lolling to one side. His hand twitches, the only sign that there's life left in his body. She presses the accelerator harder.

"Come on. Come on," she says to the car.

John groans and she looks up into the mirror.

"We're almost there," she says. "Just hang on, you hear me? Hang on."

When she looks back at the road she cries out and slams her foot on the brake. The wheels lock up and the car fishtails wildly, coming to a stop sideways across the road. She leans down in her seat to look out the window at the thing blocking her way, not ready to believe her eyes. Slowly, she opens her door and steps out, craning her neck upward.

Across the center of the road is a sheer mountain wall, hundreds of feet high. The blacktop simply runs into it and disappears as if the mountain had fallen from the sky and landed there. Looking left and right, the rock wall extends as far as she can see in either direction. Above her, the sky roils with black clouds lit by sheets of lightning.

She gets back in her car, breathing hard, a pain in her chest. She tries to put the car in drive but misses and puts it in neutral. When she hits the gas, the car gives a loud high-pitched whine.

"Come on!" she cries.

She jams it into drive, grinding the gear. The tires squeal and she nearly loses control on the soft shoulder next to the road. She corrects it and speeds down the highway. The rock wall doesn't make any sense, but she can't worry about that now. She must have missed a turn somewhere because she was going so fast. She flies back down the road, this time keeping her eyes moving, darting back and forth on both sides, only allowing herself quick looks at John.

"Almost there. I promise."

She's speeding still, but not as fast as before, not wanting to miss a turn to get her out of the forest and back to civilization. The rain starts, big, heavy drops that splatter against the windshield. She leans against her window and looks up. The storm clouds that were over the mountain are following her. The wind picks up and the trees on either side of the road pitch and twist with sudden violence. The car veers across the road and she has to correct the opposite direction, turning into the gust of wind. The clouds open up and the rain gushes, her wipers barely able to keep up. She scans each side of the road, still able to see the road to know if there's a turn-off.

But there isn't one.

She comes to the end of the pavement, the spot where the gravel road to the cabin branches off into the trees, and she stops the car. There is no way out. Not by the road anyway. As the storm howls around her, wind buffeting the car, rain hitting the metal roof like a thousand angry hands, her mind reels at the impossibility of it all.

John groans from the backseat. She hasn't the luxury to sit there and think. She has to do something.

She hits the gas and takes the road back to the cabin. Branches and leaves fall all around her, littering the road and bouncing off the hood of the car and windshield. She parks and gets out, fending off the debris thrown at her by the storm. When she opens the back door, John half-falls out and she thinks for a second that he's already dead. But when she grabs his arms she can feel him try to support himself. Together, they struggle the short distance from the car to the cabin door, the storm doing its best to knock them off their feet. Once inside, she gets him over to the living room before they fall onto the floor.

"Stop," he groans. "No more. Let me go."

She slides behind him so that she's propped up against the wall and he's cradled against her chest, her arms wrapped around him. He shudders and she closes her eyes, holding him tight. The lightning strikes are so frequent outside she can see even without a lantern on. In the bursts of light, she sees that the far wall across from her has been ripped apart, drywall and wood everywhere, the edges marked with thick claw marks. In the center of it all is the door. Closed. Light glowing around the edges.

She shakes her head. "The door. I can't do it. I can't go through it."

John manages to grab her hand. "Then you'll stay here forever."

She twists to the side so she can see his face. He leans against the wall, taking ragged, short breaths. She blinks back tears. "I want to be with you."

He smiles but it turns immediately into wincing pain. "Then you have to go," he says, looking at the door. "Y... your decision... your choice."

She stands and the cabin shakes with thunder overhead. The wind howls and it's mixed with the sound of wolves howling. She looks at the sliding glass door and sees black birds, flapping erratically with broken wings and bloodied faces as they ram themselves into the cabin. She turns back to the door and walks toward it. On the edge of her peripheral vision she sees Granger on the deck, standing in the middle of the storm, making no effort to protect himself from its fury. He's watching her but she doesn't care. Not anymore.

She reaches out, grasps the handle and opens the door. Light streams out, enveloping her, but she doesn't squint or shield her eyes. With one last look at John, she gathers all of her courage and steps through.

CHAPTER 17

Rachel sits in the passenger seat of her car, the spot meant for Underwood and Daniels. She's been here before so she's not surprised when she looks at the driver's seat and sees herself. Not a mirror image, but an actual separate version of herself humming along with the radio, fingers thumping against the steering wheel.

She spins around and chokes back a sob when she sees the passenger in the backseat. It's the boy from the woods. The boy from her writing that morning. The perfect little three-year-old that was once her son.

He's blond and tan from a summer playing outside chasing frogs, swimming in the pool, catching fireflies and riding his tricycle. His lips are turned up into a perpetual smile, like he already has life figured out. He looks right at her with his father's blue eyes and she raises her hand to say hello.

"Can you see me, Charlie?" she says. "It's momma. I'm here. Right here with you."

But Charlie can't see her and she knows it. He looks through her and out the window, his eyes tracking the rows of pine trees flashing past them. She turns to the version of herself driving the car, so clear and clean of sin, so unburdened by any real weight. She remembers the stresses of that day: the news of her lower-than-expected offer from her publisher for her next book, the worry whether they were overreaching on the brick two-story they were buying, the last conversation with her husband that had ended testy and short. All of it seemed so important that day, but none of it mattered. Not really. All of it was just the normal tugs and pushes of human existence, so transitory and meaningless that she wants to reach out and slap the furrowed brow of the woman driving the car and wake her up to the last few minutes of near perfection she would ever enjoy in her life.

"Are there gonna be other kids there?" Charlie asks.

"Probably," her other self says. Rachel hates how distracted her voice sounds, barely paying attention.

"I hope there's boys," Charlie says. "Boys are more fun."

135

"Hey, I'm fun," driving-Rachel says, giving him a little more attention.

"You're the funnest."

"Dad's pretty fun."

"Dad's the coolest. You're the funnest. And the most beautifulest."

Rachel, sitting in the passenger seat, puts her shaking hands to her mouth, trying to mask her sobs as if she was actually in the car and not simply a specter witnessing events already past.

The other Rachel smiles, just another cute moment from her son, something to store away in the memory bank. "Aww... thanks, buddy. And I think your dad is the coolest too. And the handsomest."

Charlie giggles and turns his attention back to the coloring book balanced on his lap.

The rain starts. It's not hard, that comes later. Just enough to add a thin sheen to the asphalt road. She wants to reach out and grab the wheel, yank on it to send them into the ditch. Even at full-speed it's better than what she knows is coming.

Lights flash behind them and she turns just as the other version of her looks up into the rearview mirror, adjusting it to get a better look. It's a sports car, a BMW of some kind, sleek and glistening in the light rain. It's on her ass, headlights flashing, even though they are on a two-lane road with a double-yellow line.

She hears her driver-self whisper, "Asshole," under her breath.

Up ahead the taillights of the logging truck appear in front of them. They come up to it quickly and Rachel driving the car slows down. It's going under the speed limit, a fact later determined in the investigation. Another fact later in evidence was that Reggie Perkins, the driver of the truck, was working off a hangover with the help of a bottle of bourbon and a couple of Percocet. Still, what happened wasn't because of Reggie Perkins and his lapse of judgment. Then again, maybe it was. Had he been going at least the speed limit, he would have been farther down the road when she caught up to him. Or if he'd called in sick, he never would have been on the road to begin with.

Such was the thing of any specific event, that any single thing leading up to it could have changed the trajectory of the world.

...had Reggie Perkins not grabbed a second cup of coffee that morning.

...had Rachel not changed her shirt before leaving the house.

...had the owner of the yet-to-arrive pickup truck barreling toward them been going only sixty miles an hour and not eighty-five.

...had the BMW driver waited until he'd crested the small incline before seeing what his German engineered car could do.

It was a game best played in a padded room, because none of that happened. Only the terrible thing happened. And it was about to happen again.

"Get off the road," she says to the other version of herself, her voice thin and pleading.

The red brake lights from the logging truck glare brighter in the windshield.

"Stop the car. Pull off the road." Louder now, laced with anger directed at the woman next to her who won't listen. From the corner of her eye she sees the BMW make its move, swinging out into the not-empty-for-long lane next to her.

"Pull over, you stupid bitch," she screams. "Slow down. Do something different for once. For the love of Christ, DO SOMETHING DIFFERENT!"

A blink of her eyes and she's behind the wheel.

Thank God.

She twists the wheel to pull off onto the shoulder but her hands don't move.

"No... no... no..."

She hammers the brake with her foot but nothing happens.

Then everything happens.

The BMW roars past her. She wishes she could kill the son-of-a-bitch. But she knows the pickup truck is about to take care of that for her.

Instinctively, she slows down, making space for the BMW between her and the logging truck. But the driver ignores the gesture and goes for the double-pass on the blind rise.

"What an assh—"

The words stick in her throat when she sees the truck headlights crest the hill right in front of the BMW. Things slow down and she sees every action and reaction in mind-numbing detail.

The BMW swerves right, scraping sides with the logging truck. The pickup has room to swerve to the outside, but it doesn't. It crashes head-on into the BMW, destroying the fronts of both cars with such violence that only small parts of the drivers are later found.

The truck launches up into the air over the smaller car, twisting in the air. The wreckage of the BMW jams under the logging truck, pushing it sideways. Reggie, half-asleep from the booze and painkillers, over-corrects and the cab and trailer jackknife and roll over.

Rachel hits the brake and this time it works because it's what really happened. She screams as the anti-lock brakes shudder. The undercarriage of the logging truck is in front of her like a wall across the middle of the road. She swerves but still smacks the wreckage of the BMW, careens off of it and the world turns upside down. She's weightless, flying through the air like a missile at the logging truck.

Charlie.

It's her last thought before impact.

CHAPTER 18

The crash itself is a black hole, so powerful that her mind mercifully blocks it out. When she wakes up, she's hanging upside down in her chair. The seatbelt cuts into her neck and shoulder and the airbag sags toward the ceiling. She's disoriented, confused by the lack of gravity and by what's happened to her. But that doesn't last. In a rush of panic, she remembers that her whole world is in the backseat of the car. She turns to look and the movement creates a searing burst of pain. She sees her little boy, still strapped into his car seat, face bloodied from shards of glass, head hanging to one side.

"Charlie!"

She digs at her belt buckle but it's stuck. She yanks on it, then tries to just crawl out of it. But it's locked and not moving.

Then the air catches on fire.

The first burst of flame rolls toward her like a wall as the vapors from the logging truck's punctured gas tank ignite. The deflating airbag bears the brunt of the flame, and she covers her face with her arms, gasping as the oxygen burns out from around her. The superheated air sears her skin and she screams. The flames recede but the car itself is on fire.

Desperate, she beats against her seatbelt buckle. It comes undone and she falls to the roof of the car. She drags herself out of her broken window, gulping down the fresh air outside. She crawls to the car's back door, only somewhat aware of the burned skin sloughing off her arms as she moves. Black smoke billows in her face as she pulls herself through the smashed window, oblivious to the shards of glass ripping into her legs.

Charlie's awake. Crying. And she thinks that's good because the dead don't cry. He's upside-down in his child seat, hanging in the five-point harness. That helps too since his head isn't in the smoke.

He sees her and he makes an animal sound that has the word *Momma* buried somewhere in it. He grabs for her, pulls her hair.

Her hands fumble over his car seat, her brain trying to make sense of where the straps are attached.

The fabric lining for the roof is on fire. The front seats. The air smells of gasoline and burned flesh. Her flesh.

She pulls on the straps but it just makes them tighter.

Charlie screams. Not in pain, not yet, but in pure fear. He knows the fire is coming for him.

Please God, let me save my son. Take me, just let me save my Charlie.

She presses one of the locking buttons again and this time it gives way. Charlie's left shoulder is free. If she can get the leg free, she can drag him sideways out and then...

The pain washes out her last thought. The whole left side of her catches on fire. She screams but doesn't move. Her body is all that's protecting Charlie from the flames. She reaches out for the last button. Her finger touches it, then slides off. She reaches for it again, gets her grip on it and cries out as she presses down on it.

But the second she does, she slides backward, out of the car, away from Charlie. She's outside where she can breathe, but her baby is still in the car. She crawls back to the window, but someone pulls her back. Then several pairs of strong hands have her. Good Samaritans thinking they are saving her life when really they are just killing her son.

Then the screaming starts. Impossibly loud, the sound of horrific pain.

She's on the ground, the strangers holding her there, her head against the pavement, looking right into where Charlie kicks and jerks in his car seat as the fire reaches him. She sobs as she watches her little boy, the one with the summer tan and his father's blue eyes, the one who likes to catch fireflies and ride his tricycle for hours, the one that fills her with more love than she ever thought possible. She watches as he burns alive right in front of her, screaming and kicking. And she's unable to do anything about it.

She closes her eyes and disappears into herself. The sound of the fire is still there, the smell of the smoke. Then there are sirens. Too late, always too late. They can't do anything for the little boy burned alive in the car, but they can and do save the life of the woman who lost her son.

She opens her eyes and she's in a graveyard. The sounds slowly fade away until they are in the background, only white noise. She walks next to a man and they are holding hands. When she turns, she sees that it's John. She realizes that she's known all along who he is and the charade that he was some kind of stranger at the cabin seems odd now. This is her husband. The father of their dead little boy.

She wants to say something to him, but she knows that she's still just a spectator. This has happened before. She has to see it through.

They come to a gravestone and kneel in front of it. The grass has grown over the spot where they put Charlie's charred remains all those months ago. A year was plenty of time for Mother Nature to recover from the trauma of her skin being pierced through when the grave was dug. Not so for parents grieving for their child, especially one lost in so terrible a way. They sit for a long time together, crying, holding one another. She asks for some time alone at the grave and John reluctantly gives it.

Once he's gone, she kisses her hand and places it on Charlie's headstone.

"I'm so sorry," she whispers. "So sorry."

She reaches for her purse and removes the gun from it. She looks around the world one last time, her attention oddly enough drawn to a nearby tree, reduced to bare branches by the ravages of winter. It's covered entirely by black birds who seem to watch her with interest. She smiles, then puts the gun to her head and pulls the trigger.

The shot rings out and her point of view spins violently. A blink later and she's on the ground, eyes fixed up at the sky. The black birds rise in unison from the dead tree near the grave, scattering with angry calls. Rachel feels the earth on her back, she feels the cool metal of the gun against her fingertips. She can feel these things but she can't move.

Then the ground slowly gives way. Inch by inch, she sinks down into the soft earth like she's food to be absorbed. The dry grass and leaves scratch against her cheeks as she drops deeper into soil. Her body's relaxed, no fight left in her, at peace with returning back to the darkness.

When the soil finally folds over the top of her face, it forces its way into her mouth, down her throat. The dirt drives up her nostrils, into her ears. This is when she panics. She tries to take a deep breath but can't with the pressure on her chest. She struggles against the darkness but she's packed in under the ground, buried alive.

"No!"

The scream is only in her head because her lungs are filled with dirt, but it's loud enough to shatter the world around her. The ground opens up beneath her and she falls, weightless, spinning out of control.

She lands roughly on a hard surface. She looks up and sees that she's in a white and sterile-looking hallway, lights spaced overhead in an endless series. There's a door at the end of the hallway, so far away that it's almost hard to see. It flies open and then bangs shut, like it's being blown around in a storm.

She takes a few steps toward it and the lights behind her blink out, sending the hallway behind her into total darkness. As she jogs forward, the lights continue to wink out as she passes them. She breaks into a run but the lights turning off speed up too and she can't keep up. Soon she's running in darkness, trying to catch the extinguishing lights before it's too late. With her legs burning, she sprints the final stretch, jumping at the door just as it closes.

She falls into the cabin's living room. The storm is gone, replaced by a brilliant sunny day. She turns and watches the plaster grow back over the door like it's a living thing until the door is gone and only the blank wall remains.

She gets up, looking for John. She wants to know why he didn't tell her who he was. She wants to know what he's doing in this place now that she understands what it really is.

There's a smear of blood on the floor where she left him, but he's not in the cabin. She goes outside. "John? Where are you?"

There's no answer and no sign of him. Slowly, she turns to look at Granger's cabin across the lake. She walks to the water's edge. The old man stands on the far side, binoculars up to his face, watching her.

"Granger!" she yells across the lake. Ripples spread across the surface from the power of her voice. "I know who you are. You hear me?"

Granger lowers the binoculars and tosses them to the side. They both know he doesn't need them.

"I know who you are," she yells. "And I'm coming for you."

CHAPTER 19

Rachel drags the canoe into the water and
jumps in. She paddles across the lake with her
gun on her lap, making a straight line toward
Granger. The old man stands his ground and
watches her approach.

As she digs into the water, her paddle
bounces off something solid but she ignores it. But
her next stroke strikes a mass under the surface
again and she looks over the side of the canoe to
see what it is.

The water is not the usual greenish tint; it's
dark, almost black. She pokes at the water and hits
something just under the surface. She pushes
against it and it rolls over like a log finding a new

center of gravity. As it turns, a hand breaks the surface, fingers grasping at air. An entire body bobs to the surface. She recoils and slides to the other side of the canoe. It tips and she nearly capsizes. Another body breaks the surface on the other side of her. It has a white, ghastly face, swollen from being in the water, holes eaten through its cheeks and neck.

She looks on in terror as the surface of the entire lake swells with bodies, writhing under the surface, churning the water. There are thousands of them, so thick that she could walk on them across the lake. She leans over the edge and the body nearest turns in place. It's John, eyes wide in fear, mouth open in a frozen scream.

"No!"

She reaches over the edge to grab him but he sinks back down under the press of the other bodies. Hands of decayed flesh and brittle bones reach out for her arms, trying to pull her in.

She breaks free and grabs her paddle. She digs into the piles of wet flesh around her and pulls. The canoe lurches forward, cutting through the bodies. She paddles hard and the canoe gathers speed even as she has to fight down her revulsion from the sickening, wet sounds as it cuts through skulls, ribcages and dead flesh.

Finally, she reaches the shore and climbs out of the canoe. She strides toward Granger's cabin, gun in hand. Granger stands halfway between the water and the cabin, shoulders squared to her.

But Granger isn't there alone. The cabin is covered with black birds. Wolves pace back and forth along the tree line. Snakes slither on the ground and hang from tree branches all around him. As she approaches, some of the birds burst into flames and launch screaming into the air, twisting in a manic flurry of wings before thumping to the ground.

"I know who you are," she yells.

Granger looks unconcerned. "What do you think you know?"

She raises the gun and fires five shots into the man's chest, striding toward him the entire time. His body jerks with each impact, but there's no blood. When she stops shooting, he stands up straight and holds out his hands, smiling.

"If you knew who I was, then you wouldn't be bothering with that gun," he says.

She throws the gun aside and walks up to him until they stand toe-to-toe.

"I know exactly who you are. You're the Devil."

He smiles. "Not my favorite name, but it will suffice. Beelzebub. Shaitan. Memnoch. So many more poetic options."

Without warning she slaps him across the face. She connects hard enough that it turns his head and stings her palm. She's surprised she made contact and, for a split second, she sees that the Devil is surprised too. When he turns his head back to her, the arrogant sneer on his face has transformed into a menacing snarl.

149

"Do that again and you'll regret it."

"What are you going to do with me?" She gestures all around them. "Send me to Hell? Trap me in purgatory for all eternity? I'm already there." She lashes out again, but this time he's ready for her. He grabs her wrist painfully.

"It can be worse," he says. "It can be infinitely worse, believe me."

She pulls her hand back but her anger is now doused with a good measure of fear.

"Why do you think you're here?" the Devil asks.

She hears the sound of fire and sirens. "I remember…" she says. "I remember everything."

The Devil steps closer, their faces almost touching. He eyes her like she's a specimen to be studied.

"Then tell me why you're here," the Devil says.

"Where's John?" she asks. "Where's my husband?"

The Devil looks surprised and doesn't even try to hide it. "Interesting. Perhaps you do remember." Then his voice turns hard. "Tell me why you're here."

"I killed myself. I killed… I killed someone I love. That's why I'm here. There's a circle of Hell just for people like me. That's why I'm being punished."

"And why did you kill yourself?"

"My son…"

"What about him?"

"He's dead."

"You said you killed someone you loved. Was it him?"

Silence.

"Was it him? Did you kill him?"

"Yes."

"Then you're here because of that?"

Silence.

"How'd you do it? How'd you kill him?"

Nothing.

"With your hands?"

"No."

"With a weapon then. A knife. A baseball bat maybe?"

"Nothing like that. He was... he was trapped. We were both trapped. There was an accident..."

The Devil spits on the ground at her feet. The ground sizzles and burns where it hits. "An accident? I thought you said you killed him."

"I didn't... I didn't save him." Her voice cracks and her eyes sting as the tears come. She doesn't try to stop them. "I watched him die... right in front of me... and I didn't save him. What kind of mother does that?"

The Devil pulls out a bottle from his pocket. As he does the wolves prowling the property howl in unison. She stares at the bottle as the Devil shakes it from side to side.

"You know what this is, don't you? It's what we talked about before. Drink this and you can forget everything. The accident. The fire. All of that pain that nearly killed you. Just strip it away. The burden of that memory isn't bearable, so why even try?"

"I can't."

"You can feel whole again. Don't you want that?"

She squeezes her eyes shut but all she can see is her son's final seconds in the fire. All she can hear is his screams.

"It'll be like none of it ever happened," the Devil says. "So easy. Just one drink."

She opens her eyes but her son's screaming is still in her head.

"Don't you want to end the pain?"

"Yes," she whispers. "God, yes, I do."

She reaches for the bottle, but the Devil pulls it away from her at the last second.

"One last question," he says. "What was your son's name?"

She shakes her head. It's too much. Too painful. It feels like there's a knife in her gut. "Just let me have the bottle. *Please.*"

The Devil grins as he holds the bottle back out. "Maybe you have suffered enough." He lets her take the bottle from his hand. "Take it and drink. It'll all be better soon. It'll be like your son never existed."

The bottle is halfway to her lips when she stops. She closes her eyes and pictures her son's face. Sees him playing with John, laughing as they chase each other on the back lawn. She hears his sweet voice, so light and pure that her heart nearly breaks. She cradles her arms as she stands there and she swears she can feel his weight there as she rocks him to sleep.

"Can you answer the question?" the Devil asks. "What was your son's name?"

"Charlie," she says. "My son's name was Charlie."

"And how did Charlie die?"

"A car accident. He burned in a fire."

"Did you kill Charlie?" the Devil asks.

She sways on her feet, her eyes still closed. She can see Charlie in the backseat of the car, upside down, flames engulfing him. But there are no sirens. No smell of smoke.

"Was it your fault?"

She shakes her head.

"Say it," he says.

She opens her eyes and the Devil is in front of her. Only now his eyes are kind and gentle. In a softer voice, he says, "Rachel, can you say the words?"

"It wasn't my fault," she whispers. She turns the bottle and drains the contents onto the ground. "It wasn't my fault." The bottle drops from her fingers. "His name was Charlie and I want to remember him." She looks up to the Devil's eyes. "It's worth any price to be able to remember him."

The Devil reaches out and takes her hands in his, his eyes searching hers. He gives her a reassuring squeeze.

"You know what? I think you're right," he says. "It is worth it."

A silent moment stretches out between them and she enjoys the blissful silence of her quieted mind.

"You did very well. Very well." He lets go of one of her hands and pulls her carefully with the other like they were the best of friends going for a stroll. "Now I want you to rest for a while." He guides her over to a chair. "Just for a few minutes. Can you do that?"

She sits in the offered chair, numb and exhausted. She's not sure what just happened, but she's too tired to try to work it out. The Devil seems pleased with her cooperation.

"Good," he says. "Wait here and I'll be back. I have a surprise for you."

He turns and walks to his cabin. The Devil searches his pockets for something, gives up and then knocks on the cabin door. A few seconds later, the door opens and the Devil disappears inside.

She glances around her. All of the Devil's creatures are gone. No more wolves or snakes. Or screaming black birds that burst into flames. The sun is high in the sky and warms her skin. A slight breeze carries the scent of pine and wild huckleberry to her. She listens to the birdsong and the sounds of the trees doing their slow dance in the wind. She feels completely at peace. A broken heart to be sure, the terror of what happened to her son still there, but a memory now, not something relived by the smallest trigger. Her heart aches for her son and she knows it always will. But her mind is quiet. At long last.

Then she notices something shiny in the grass at her feet. She bends over and picks up a key. She thinks that the Devil must have dropped it before he left, which is curious. She stands up and looks around, half-expecting him to appear and ask for it back. But it's just her there. She turns the key over in her hand, wondering if she's better off just putting it back in the grass where she found it. But curiosity is a powerful thing and she closes her fist around the key.

She walks to the Devil's cabin and inspects the door. It looks different from the last time she was there. Now it's made of old, weathered boards hung vertically with rusted iron bands holding it together. The handle is a gnarled piece of tree root that looks like an arthritic finger. Right above the door handle is a shiny metal plate, the size of a silver dollar, with a keyhole in the center.

She reaches out and slides the key into the hole and turns.

Click.

The door unlocks and edges open half an inch.

She hesitates, some part of her brain trying to warn her away from what she's about to do. But she doesn't listen. She opens the door with the key that she was never meant to find and enters a world she was not yet meant to see.

Chapter 20

The last time she walked into Granger's cabin it was a single dark room filled with trash and stuffed dead animals. But all of that's gone now. It's not even a room on the other side of the door now, but a brightly lit hallway with a linoleum floor and immaculate white walls.

The door has changed too. It's no longer wood but a sleek metal door with white enamel paint. There's a small rectangular window in the center but it's blocked by a piece of black cardboard taped on the outside of the door. Panicked, she steps back and pulls the door shut, hoping that it will transform back into the wooden door. But it doesn't. It stays metal and, in a rush of understanding, she realizes that it's been that way the entire time.

Slowly, she turns around and looks behind her.

She's in a windowless room. Her room. There's a metal frame bed with white sheets and a grey wool comforter, the same kind that she laid outside at her own cabin the night she made love to John under the stars.

Under the stars...

Above her, stuck to the white plaster ceiling, are dozens of star-shaped stickers, the glow-in-the-dark kind used in kids' rooms. Her eyes track down to the table at the foot of the bed. In the center of the table is Underwood in all of his gleaming glory with a stack of blank paper and a large water bottle next to it. She walks over to the table and picks up the bottle. Scratched in her own handwriting on a piece of paper taped to the bottle are the words *Jack Daniels* along with a crude drawing of the label. She unscrews the cap and smells the contents, confirming what she suspected. Just water. As she puts it back on the table, she notices two chairs around a pile of rolled up pieces of paper stacked up to look like a campfire.

But it is the far wall that really draws her attention. Floor to ceiling, the wall is covered with drawings. The middle of the wall has a large swath of butcher paper taped to it but the crude sketches continue off the paper and onto the walls themselves. She walks to the wall, her fingers tracing the images. Massive wolves. Hundreds of black birds, some of them on fire. A lake surface with hands reaching out. And in the center of it all, in the middle of the wall, are drawings of a door. Drawn and then scratched out. Drawn and scratched out. Over and over until there are gouges through the paper and into the wall itself.

She suddenly feels claustrophobic. She turns in place and notices leather restraints attached to the bedframe. She spins again, dizzy now, and she knows she has to get out of the room. On the way to the door she steps on a toy plastic gun and it cracks under her bare foot. That's when she notices that she's not wearing the clothes she thought, but sweatpants and a loose t-shirt. She reaches up to her head and nearly screams from what she feels there.

Her hair is gone. Her scalp feels rough and strange beneath her fingers. Slowly, she moves her hands down her forehead and over her face. It's the same rough skin as her scalp. She looks around the room for a mirror but there isn't one. In fact, she can't find any reflective surface at all.

There's a pain in her chest and it feels like the air has run out. She has to get out of the room. Twisting the key again, she opens the door and bursts through into the hallway. It's a long corridor with closed metal doors on either side, each with a window in the middle of it. A few are covered with black paper like hers. She chooses one of these on the opposite side of the hallway and raises it up.

There's a man inside, sitting on the floor, his arms wrapped around his shoulders as he sways back and forth in an invisible wind. His mouth moves in a torrent of unspoken words while a line of spittle hangs from the edge of his mouth and drips down his chin. She puts the paper back into place and moves to the next door.

This one is padded and its occupant is a woman in a loose-fitting restraint, not as restrictive as a straightjacket, but enough to limit her arm movements. Even though the woman is standing on the far wall opposite from the door, she's observant and notices Rachel looking into her room. The woman smiles and nods, the way she might if they were acquaintances passing one another in a supermarket aisle. Rachel waves back. Then the woman launches herself across the room, screaming. She rams the window with her forehead. On reflex, Rachel jerks backward and drops the piece of black paper back over the window. She carefully slides it back to the side and sees a smear of blood on the glass. Craning forward, she sees the woman sprawled on the floor, half-conscious.

"I once was lost, but now am found..." comes a voice from down the hallway.

She recognizes the voice. She searches for a hiding spot but there isn't one.

"Was blind, but now I see..."

She doesn't want to do it, but she knows if she stays in the hallway she'll be caught. And, once caught, she'll be back in the room and her shiny key will be taken away. So she runs to her room and goes back inside, but not before ripping down the piece of black paper covering the window on her door.

She double-checks that she still has her key before she pulls the door closed behind her until the lock clicks into place. Then she looks out the window until Ollie comes into view, still singing. He's behind a janitor's cart, the kind with two garbage receptacles on it and spots for a variety of mops and brooms. Her mind's clicking now. She remembers meeting Ollie in the forest as he was sweeping the path of leaves. Only he hadn't been sweeping leaves, she realizes. He'd been sweeping the hallways, his opinions about Sisyphean tasks still holding true.

She waits until Ollie passes and then sneaks back out into the hallway. She turns right, the opposite direction of where Ollie just headed, and makes her way to the end of the hallway until she hits a T intersection. She hears voices, raised and angry coming from a room to the left and she goes that direction, staying close to the wall like she's a cat burglar in some old movie.

"...then why can't I see her?"

She freezes. It's John. Not shot in the stomach. Not dead in a lake full of bodies. But alive. Her impulse is to run to him, but something holds her back. She wants to know what is going on. She creeps closer until she's right outside the door. Most importantly, there is a second door only a few steps away marked SUPPLY giving her an escape if she needs it.

"...gotten this far on my advice, why are you questioning me now?" It is the Devil's voice. No, she thinks to herself. That wasn't right.

She looks at the bronze plaque on the wall right next to her, so close that she has to take a step back from the wall to get a better look at it.

Dr. Horace Granger, PhD
Director of Psychiatry

"Your wife had a breakthrough today," Granger says. "Reintroducing you into the mix could set her back."

"It was when I was with her that things got better. After we... after I stayed with her overnight..."

She hears Granger make a disapproving grunt. "No, that just made her burrow deeper into her imaginary world. She would have stayed there forever if you let her, playing house at her imaginary lake cabin with the man who rented it to her."

"Maybe that would be better," John whispers. "Maybe she could have been happy."

"But it wouldn't be real. She'd be living a fantasy."

"And just what the hell's so great about reality?"

She hears the pain in his voice, but she still resists the temptation to go to him.

"Today was a good day," Granger says. "Your wife has fabricated an amazing world, more intricate than anything I've ever seen before. It's an amalgamation of the trauma she experienced from the accident, her real-world interactions here like her meeting with the janitor Ollie, and her knowledge of literature. She has layered aspects of the circles of hell from *Dante's Inferno* into her constructed reality. It's quite amazing."

"She did her thesis on Dante," John says.

"Yes, it was in her file from the previous doctor," Granger says. "It explains the lake of damned souls, the black wolves, the purgatory for suicides where Dante says the damned are endlessly hunted by harpies. And in her mind she assigned me the role of the Devil. She believes I'm the one punishing her for her sin."

"Which you played up."

"This is my process. You knew it was unconventional when you applied to bring her here."

There's a long pause. She closes her eyes and leans heavily against the wall, trying to process what she's hearing.

"So what happened today?" John finally asks.

"She came back from her world enough to remember the accident. To remember your son's death. Even so, she still put me in to the role of the Devil persecuting her. Because of this she believed that I had the power to deliver on my promise to have her forget your son and his death. Even with that belief, she chose not to forget. That's a powerful thing."

"It would be a blessing if she could forget," John says.

"If you could erase your memory of the death of your son only by forgetting he ever existed, would you?"

There's another long pause. "No, of course not," John says, but he doesn't sound very convincing.

"There's more," Granger says. "When I made you leave her room, in her mind, it was like I'd killed you. Even after you were out of the room, she went on for a long time talking about you being shot and bleeding. Then she went quiet, like she went somewhere deep inside herself. When she came out, she remembered you as her husband."

"Wait... what did you just say?"

"She remembers you," Granger says. "Not as the man who rented the cabin to her, but as her husband and father to your son. What we need to do is... wait... you can't see her yet."

She darts back to the small space in front of the closet just as the door to Granger's office opens. John strides out followed by Granger, only he looks nothing like the man she has come to know. He wears a coat and tie and his grey hair is neatly combed back against his scalp. He chases after John. If either of them turn, they'll see her halfway into the hallway. Neither of them do.

"Rachel!" John calls out, running down the hallway now.

"She's too fragile," Granger calls after him. "We have to move slowly. It could be dangerous."

They turn the corner and their voices fade. She runs into Granger's office and closes the door behind her, breathing hard, her head spinning. The office is immaculate with furniture placed in perfect symmetry for the space. There's an oiled hardwood desk with three pens lined up next to a blank pad of paper. A deer head hangs on one wall and the other has two stuffed pheasants made to look like they are in midflight.

She runs to the window, the urge to escape her prison almost overwhelming her. Even the prospect of seeing John doesn't slow her down. They're holding her against her will. She needs to get away. Nothing else matters.

She sees that she's on the first floor of the building. Right outside is a patch of grass that slopes down to a parking lot. It's her chance. She turns and yanks open Granger's desk drawers one by one, rummaging through the neatly organized contents. Nothing. She searches the surface of the desk but still no sign of what she's looking for.

She glances up and sees a porcelain dish on the table right by the door to the office. A set of keys rests on top of a pile of change. Jackpot. She runs over and grabs the key fob attached with an Audi insignia on it. That will make it easier to find the car.

She runs to the window, flips the locks and jerks it open. She crawls up on the windowsill and swings her feet over until they dangle next to the red brick wall. The fall down to the grass looks father than she expected and she hesitates.

The office door flies open behind her. John and Granger run in.

"Rachel!" John says. "Stop. Wait."

She wants to wait. She wants to swing her legs back over and feel his arms around her. But she knows that if she stays they'll put her back in the room with the drawings on the wall and the restraints on the bed. She can't do that.

Just as a hand grabs her, she pushes off the window and drops to the ground. She hits hard and shoulder rolls forward. She doesn't risk looking back because she knows they will come after her. She runs as hard as she can to the parking lot, clicking the key fob as she runs. A car chirps. Not an Audi, but a red Honda. She doesn't care. It's just a way for her to escape what's chasing her and that's all that matters.

She climbs in, starts the car and punches the gas. The tires squeal as she races out of the parking lot and onto the main road. She's filled with a sense of victory at her escape and excitement at her new freedom. But then she looks in the rearview mirror and screams at the sight of her own face.

She's bald, a jagged scar showing the spot she'd destroyed with her suicide attempt. But that isn't the worst of it. Her face is gone. No nose or mouth. Not even ears on the sides of her head. Just the slick shine of a burn victim's skin stretched tight across her skull and her eyes staring back in the mirror from inside the monster's face.

With a cry, she slaps the rearview mirror away with the back of her hand. The car swerves and she nearly loses control. She corrects and the car swings back onto the road before she slams on the brakes. The car skids to a stop in the center of the empty street. She gasps for air, in a full anxiety attack, her eyes squeezed shut trying to block out the image from the mirror.

Slowly, she settles down and catches her breath. It can't be true. The image couldn't have been her. Carefully, she reaches to touch her face. It feels like normal skin to her now. She feels eyebrows. And then her nose. She turns the mirror back to her.

It's her face. The one she knows is really her. Without burns. Without parts missing. She touches the long brown hair that falls to her shoulders and pulls it back into a ponytail. She readjusts the rearview mirror so she can see the road behind her, long and straight, bordered on either side by tall pines. She notices black clouds churning in the air behind her. Ahead of her, the road looks identical, only without the dark clouds.

A faint *clink-clink* sounds next to her. Underwood and Jack, her two eternal companions, are strapped together in the passenger seat, ready for anything. She smiles, thinking that buckling them together might have been overdoing it, but it makes her laugh, so she forgives herself the indulgence. This is her journey, her time, so acting odd is her prerogative.

She knows she's making a terrible mistake, but that's never stopped her before. Even as she speeds down the empty highway, she's certain nothing good will come of this trip. She can't say why she has this belief, only that it's deeply rooted, part of a visceral animal instinct clawing away at her insides. Call it intuition. Or call it common sense, doesn't matter. Doesn't change the fact that it's the truth.

She refuses to change her destination, even if her rising sense of dread causes her heart to beat right out of her chest. She's committed, this much is a fact, so she pushes aside all thought of turning around and focuses on the road ahead.

Before long, she pulls into the driveway of the cabin. There's a bull's skull standing guard, bleached white by the sun. She knocks on the door to no answer so she walks along the side of the house toward the water.

"Can I help you?" a man's voice says to her left.

She's so taken by the view that she doesn't even turn.

"I don't think you can," she whispers.

"Will you let me try?"

She turns to the man walking toward her and meets his eyes.

"Yes," she says. "Please."

Author's Note

Dear Reader,

Thank you three times.

First, thank you for supporting a fellow human being's passion. I think it makes you a good person and makes up for that one thing you did in high school (you know what I'm talking about).

Second, thank you for being part of the community of readers. Each time you write a review, recommend a book to a friend or share a new novel through social media, you help keep the fire for books alive. Those of us who scribble stories late into the night are completely in your debt. If you can write even a short review right now when the book is fresh in your mind, it would be greatly appreciated.

Lastly, thank you for your time. As a father of five and an avid reader (labels that can seem mutually exclusive at times), I recognize every book you open represents a hard choice among thousands of options. I'm awed and humbled that you chose to spend your valuable time within these pages. I hope that I proved to be worthy of your trust.

Readers have asked me more often about my inspiration for RACHEL AMES than for any other book. Many wonder if I'm trying to process a personal tragedy in my own life through these pages. Fortunately, that is not the case.

However, readers may notice the recurrence of children-in-jeopardy throughout my books. This was not intentional but just how my mind works. As a dad, I can think of nothing more devastating or irrecoverable as the loss of a child. I'm so protective and so fearful for my five kids that if I didn't exorcise some of my demons on these pages, I don't think I could bear it.

For those readers who have experienced the pain of losing a child, some of who have written to me that they can relate the madness on the pages here, my entire heart goes out to you. It's said time heals all wounds. I don't know if that's true or not, but I like to think that it is and that even the grieving father or mother can somehow find calm and peace in their world again. That is my hope and prayer.

With appreciation,

Jeff Gunhus

Acknowledgements

Every book is a journey that starts alone and, if the writer is lucky, ends up a gathering of trusted friends and talented people. So many helped with this novella. Mandy Schoen's keen eye and developmental notes strengthened the book tremendously. My new assistant Kate Tilton was an early beta reader and likely wondered just what she'd gotten herself into by working with me. But she was great and had smart, insightful comments. Other early readers that impacted the book included Tracy Meneses, Jason Reid, Jim Beard and Robb Cadigan (who also put up with me badgering him about potential book titles.) If there's something you find lacking in the telling of this story, the failing is mine as one of the people above likely pointed it out to me at some point.

Thank you also to Carly Hoffmann and the team at Kindle Singles. I was honored that you found merit in this novella and allowed me to occupy the same space as some of my heroes that influenced my work like Stephen King, Dean Koontz and Hugh Howey. Also, a special thank you to Steve Berry for his full day master craft class he taught at Thrillerfest in New York. I rewrote most of this novella after that class. It was the single more impactful day on my writing. Thank you.

Lastly, thank you to my friends and family who put up my distractions and my odd stories. To my kids who must think their father is odd getting up at 5 AM to bang away on a laptop. And most of all a thank you to my wife and best friend Nicole. Everyone ought to have someone who dusts off your knees when you fall and tells you to get back in the game no matter the score, and that's what Nicole does for me. Without her love and support, none of it works.

Thank you all.

Best,

Jeff Gunhus

About The Author

Jeff Gunhus is the author of the Amazon bestselling supernatural thrillers, *Night Chill* and *Night Terror* and the thriller *Killer Within*. He also writes the middle grade/YA series, *The Templar Chronicles*. The first book of the series, *Jack Templar Monster Hunter*, was written in an effort to get his reluctant reader eleven-year-old son excited about reading. It worked and a new series was born. His book *Reaching Your Reluctant Reader* has helped hundreds of parents create avid readers. As a father of five, he and his wife Nicole spend most of their time chasing kids and taking advantage of living in the great state of Maryland. In rare moments of quiet, he can be found in the back of the City Dock Cafe in Annapolis working on his next novel. If you see him there, sit down and have a cup of coffee with him. You just might end up in his next book.

www.JeffGunhus.com

www.facebook.com/jeffgunhusauthor
www.twitter.com/jeffgunhus

Made in the USA
San Bernardino, CA
20 November 2015